"So that's your secret mission?"

Annie's voice was barely audible. She felt sick knowing Brett had a special assignment with the local sheriff, an assignment that could lead Brett straight to her door.

"Look, Annie, I'm sure I don't need to tell you to keep this quiet," Brett said. "My goal is to apprehend these offenders, and if word gets out . . ."

Annie listened mesmerized. She could see Brett's enthusiasm grow as he talked about his project. And every word filled her with more guilt and misery. Obviously he thought he could trust her—especially after the love they'd just shared.

He frowned and studied her expression. "Are you okay? You aren't disturbed by all this talk about criminals, are you?"

"Of course not," she lied. She knew she couldn't tell him. Not now. It seemed she was getting in deeper and deeper. And as she heard his next words, a chill ran through her.

"Sometimes," he was saying, "even the most innocent are not what they seem. . . ."

Mary Tate Engels first introduced Annie Clayton to readers in her fourth Temptation, *Best-Laid Plans*. But Annie was too intriguing a character to stay in the background for long. So Mary made Annie the heroine of her own Temptation, *Ripe for the Picking*. Besides, Mary *loves* apples and always imagined it would be heaven to live on an apple farm, just like Annie. During her research, Mary discovered there are excellent orchards in New Mexico, close enough to Mary's Arizona home to consider them in her own backyard. And close enough to visit and sample the "flavor" of her novel's setting!

Books by Mary Tate Engels

HARLEQUIN TEMPTATION
243—THE RIGHT TIME
267—BEST-LAID PLANS

Writing as Corey Keaton

HARLEQUIN TEMPTATION
194—THE NESTING INSTINCT

Don't miss any of our special offers. Write to us at the following address for information on our newest releases.

Harlequin Reader Service
901 Fuhrmann Blvd., P.O. Box 1397, Buffalo, NY 14240
Canadian address: P.O. Box 603,
Fort Erie, Ont. L2A 5X3

Ripe for the Picking

MARY TATE ENGELS

Harlequin Books

TORONTO • NEW YORK • LONDON
AMSTERDAM • PARIS • SYDNEY • HAMBURG
STOCKHOLM • ATHENS • TOKYO • MILAN

Thanks to the apple growers
of Wilcox, Arizona
for information on the exciting
and not-so-easy business of producing apples.

And to Madeline and Darrell
for mariachi *espectáculos* and *pozole*
and great fun enjoying both!

Published April 1990

ISBN 0-373-25395-8

1

ANNIE CLAYTON LIFTED her head and listened. She sensed something strange in the air; she wasn't sure what. A change in the weather? Or was someone watching her?

The wind caught her unruly hair, tossing it carelessly, and although the air was cool, the high New Mexico sun caught its red and gold highlights, creating a glittering halo about her head.

She heard a footstep...or thought she did. She halted. Silence...except for the wind that whispered to the crumbling adobe bricks and ran off laughing.

Standing very still, Annie closed her eyes. Diego always said these eerie sensations came from the spirits, *los espíritus*. But Diego was old and had funny ideas. With a shiver, Annie opened her eyes and took a few more steps toward the crumbling mission ruins.

She could see nothing out of the ordinary. It was the same, always the same, as it had been for two hundred years. The old Spanish mission site, located in the far corner of her property, exuded a strange aura. So strange, in fact, that only a few ventured there. At one time, Uncle Martin had threatened to tear the building down, but Aunt Annalee had persuaded him to leave it standing.

Today the sensations seemed especially strong to Annie. Maybe it was the pending storm. Or *los espíritus* as Diego claimed.

After Aunt Annalee died, Diego believed she had joined *los espíritus* of the mission. Annie sighed and leaned against the tumbledown building, her shoulders absorbing heat from the sun-warmed bricks. Or perhaps it was Aunt Annalee's spirit warming her. That's what she preferred to believe, in her desire to perpetuate the beautiful memory of a lady she had loved very much.

Annie sometimes came here for a very private conversation with Aunt Annalee . . . or whoever would listen. "I'm worried about this storm that's coming," she said aloud. "It's a bad time of year for a frost. The trees have full blossoms for the first time in several years, and I can't lose them now. If I'm going to hang on to the farm, I have to have a profitable year soon."

She waited. There were no answers. She didn't really expect any. The only sound came from the wind whistling around the crumbling adobe. Then, out of the silence, one word seemed to emerge . . . *help . . . help.*

"Help? Sure. I'll need help, all right, if this storm brings the frost they're predicting. There's always Diego. He's the only one available this time of year. It's too early for the migrants. But he's not strong enough to be much help anymore."

She paused to listen again, but the world was silent. Finally Annie made her way back to the red-and-white Jeep where Feliz waited. The curious dalmation, who normally followed Annie everywhere, wouldn't budge when they came out here. Diego said it because of *los espíritus.*

Annie gave the ancient place one last look, feeling the spirits' eyes on her retreating back.

ANNIE MUSCLED the sturdy Jeep between the ruts in the unpaved road that edged the neighboring Meyer ranch. Drawn by the sight of the familiar white pickup truck with its red and blue lights on top, she turned under the Rocking M sign and drove into the weed-infested driveway.

Parking behind the truck, she waved to the tall, lean man standing on the porch. "Hi, stranger," she called. "We don't see much of you around here anymore."

"Hey, Annie." He motioned for her to join him.

J.M. Meyer had moved to town several years ago, after his wife, Rosa, died and their only son showed no interest in ranching. It seemed a shame to Annie that he left this perfectly fine ranch to deteriorate, but J.M. seldom came out to the old homestead anymore, especially since being elected county sheriff.

When she reached the steps, he shook her hand and grinned. "Apple farming must agree with you, Annie. I've never seen you looking prettier."

She shook her head at his compliment. She knew her hair was a mess and she'd been too busy to bother with makeup today. "It's a good life, if you can make ends meet, but we miss you out here. Thinking about moving back? I'd love to have a neighbor again."

"Good. Because Brett's going to try his hand at a slower pace for a change. I came out to see how bad the place looked." He chuckled softly as his gaze swept the house with its peeling paint and overgrown yard. "Pretty bad."

"How's Brett doing?"

"He's out of the hospital, but still needs some time to fully recover."

"So he's coming here to recuperate?"

"Yep. He wasn't happy with his new assignment. After his injury, the FBI wanted him to take a desk job in D.C. That didn't sit well with him, so he's considering getting out altogether. That wouldn't bother me. It's a damned dangerous business. I suggested that he come back and try ranching for a while. This is a good place to live, don't you think?"

"It is for me. But I'm sure it's a far cry from the excitement of Miami and working with the FBI." She figured J.M. must have done some fast talking to get his son to come back to New Mexico. "There's a lot of work to be done around here if he intends to turn this into a working ranch again."

J.M. shoved his white cowboy hat back on his head. "Brett can pace himself and take it easy until he feels like working harder. I always figured that work was good for a man, especially one who has a lot of thinking to do."

"Guess it's good for a woman, too, J.M." Annie clamped one hand on her hair as a gust of wind whipped it around her face. "I find myself working harder and harder to make a go of it. I just don't want to admit defeat."

"You'll do it, Annie. Takes time. Old Martin let the place go to hell the past few years, so you took over a big mess." He gestured at the front yard. "Just like Brett will have to do. He doesn't know it's this bad. In fact, I didn't know it was such a wreck."

"It's pretty bad," she agreed. "My problem is that I'm running out of time and money. I have to produce a crop this season. I can't handle another deficit year. And if this storm is anything like what they're predicting, a frost will nip the first healthy blossoms I've seen in several years."

"Aw, it probably won't be as bad as the forecasts. The weathermen tend to exaggerate whatever appears on their dang computer screens. It's rare to get a heavy frost this late in April."

"You forget I come from California—weather there isn't so predictable."

"Well, if it comes, I'll be the first one out here to set up the smudge pots. You'll need lots of help."

"Thanks, J.M. It's nice to know I can count on the sheriff for assistance as well as protection. Well, I'd better get busy. Nice to see you again, J.M. And tell your son welcome back for me."

"Will do. I'm sure I'll be around more often, now that Brett's coming home, Annie."

"Great."

She drove away, thinking about Brett Meyer. She'd only seen him a few times in all the summers she'd spent on her aunt and uncle's apple farm. When they were young, she paid little attention to the skinny boy on the next ranch. All she remembered about him was that he had jet-black hair and mahogany eyes, from his Mexican mother. And when she was old enough to care, he had been away at military school or college or finally, working for the FBI. When he returned for Rosa's funeral, he had kept to himself, enduring his grief in privacy. She respected that.

A couple of months ago, Annie and the tiny town of Silverton, New Mexico, had been shocked to hear the name of their sheriff's son on the nightly news. Brett Meyer had been shot and severely wounded in a drug bust in Miami. He nearly died.

J.M. had flown to Brett's side at the Miami hospital, and the next week, he had returned to brag that his son had received a commendation from the vice president. J.M. was justifiably proud of his son, a local boy who'd made good.

THE NEXT DAY Annie's activity in the orchards increased. *Los ojos* watched anxiously.

She lifted the metal smudge pot from the back of her Jeep and hauled it clumsily across the irrigation ditch. She had no thoughts of spirits or anything else besides the frost on her precious apple trees.

The tiny pink-white blossoms on skinny bare branches were totally vulnerable at this stage. The forecast promised below-freezing temperatures tonight, a late April storm that could wipe out Annie's entire apple crop for the year. Would those beautiful, little full-of-hope blooms droop and turn brown by midmorning tomorrow?

Por Dios! Not if she could help it!

Determinedly Annie tugged another smudge pot to the line of trees. In theory, the heavy smoke from the kerosene heaters would act as a cloud to insulate the orchard. Actually the smoke raised the temperature only a few degrees, but that was often enough to save a crop.

When she turned around she was just in time to see J.M.'s truck parking near her Jeep. God bless J.M....he'd said he'd come to help. She smiled gratefully and waved.

The man who emerged from the truck, however, wasn't Sheriff J.M. Meyer. Oh, he was lean and long legged like J.M. But his jeans were definitely tighter, and he had no Stetson. When he hopped the irrigation ditch his step was light. He wore brown walking boots, which she noticed because they weren't typical of the cowboy boots most of the local men wore, and they were spotlessly clean. Nobody around here stayed that clean for long.

As he approached she could see that he was as tall as the sheriff but much darker. His shock of hair was jet black and cut short around the ears, longer in back. Intense ebony eyes, a coppery complexion and the straight-nosed, thin-lipped face hinted at Spanish and Indian ancestors. He was J.M.'s son all right, but his resemblance favored his beautiful Mexican mother.

"Hi. My dad said you'd need some help tonight."

"I sure do," she replied. "By nightfall I'll need all the help I can get." She gazed appreciatively at the man reputed to be a hero. Neither handsome nor good-looking properly described him. Perhaps princely or noble more appropriately applied. "You must be Brett."

"And you, Annie." He extended a large hand. "My, have I heard a lot about you."

"You're the one who made the TV news." Her work-roughened hand was lost in the strength and noticeable smoothness of his. "And the front page of the *Silverton Gazette*. You're quite a hero around here."

"It's because of my dad. Otherwise, it was just another drug-related incident."

"J.M.'s mighty proud of you. And from what I've read in the newspapers, he has every right to be." For the first time in ages she wished she'd worn work gloves and taken better care of her hands. Self-consciously she slid them into her jacket pockets.

"They both exaggerate." He tossed his head back in a dismissive gesture. The motion reminded her of a stallion chomping at the bit. "I'm a man who happened to be unlucky enough to get in the way of a couple of bullets. That's no hero."

"But you were doing a hero's job, trying to capture criminals. That's pretty fine work to most folks."

"You know what the FBI does for their heroes who get shot?" His dark eyes hardened. "They give you a large desk in a fancy office. That's why I'm here now and not still on the job."

"Where you'd rather be, I take it?"

"You bet. I gave them ten good years and nearly my life. They gave me a commendation from the veep and my choice of a window or aisle desk."

"Somebody's got to keep the organization running."

"Well, it won't be me. I'd rather—" he paused and motioned to the four-foot-high metal heater "—be hauling smudge pots. Which is why I'm here."

"The FBI's loss is our gain." She propped her fists on slim hips and glanced over the orchard behind her. "You're exactly what I need tonight. It's too early for the migrants, so all I have is Diego."

"Diego's still here? He must be a hundred years old by now."

"Not quite. He's seventy and still going strong, except for his arthritic hip. He worked for Uncle Martin more than thirty years and sure does know his apples. I couldn't get along without him. But on occasion, I do need someone a little stronger." She gave Brett a sassy grin. "And you look like you'll fill the bill."

"Might as well use me while I'm here. What's first?"

"I need all the smudge pots distributed around the outer perimeter and at twenty-foot intervals along the inside rows."

"Okay, where are they?"

"The rest of them are stored in the shed near the house." She started toward the two vehicles, which were parked nose to nose. "Diego's taken our truck for fuel. I'm glad you brought J.M.'s truck. Mind if we use it for hauling the smokers?"

"I figured it would come in handy." Brett fell into step with her. "That's why I drove it instead of my car." Actually he knew his Mercedes would draw attention, and he preferred to delay dealing with the locals.

"Is J.M. coming?"

"I doubt it. He and his deputy took the police car to check out a report of a truckful of illegal aliens near the county line."

"Now, that sounds more like your kind of job, Brett." She stepped across the irrigation ditch. Her boots, she noticed, were caked with mud, in sharp contrast to Brett's shiny ones.

"Maybe it is, but I'm here to do a job for you, Annie. And I intend to give it my all."

"The temperature usually drops after one in the morning. I plan to keep an all-night vigil."

"Then, so will I."

"It'll be a rough, cold night," she warned, pulling her jacket tighter.

"I've had plenty of those."

"Most folks just come to help for a few hours. It'll be okay if you decide to leave." She didn't want to impose.

"Not a chance. I'm here for the duration." Brett had to admit his dad was right about Annie Clayton. She was a beauty. With that wild strawberry hair and those sea-green eyes, she struck him as an attractive woman who, under other circumstances, could be fun. If he stuck around until the circumstances changed, Annie might just be worth the wait. She was certainly a woman with spunk, and that appealed to him. "We'll vigil together, Annie."

"You don't have anything more important to do on your first night back in town?"

He grinned. His teeth appeared brilliantly white against his tanned complexion, and Annie became fully aware of his masculine appeal. "I didn't know there was any nightlife in Silverton."

"It's changed, but not that much," she said with a scoff. "Maybe filling smudge pots will be the most exciting thing to happen on a night like this."

"Then let's get with it." He hunched his shoulders against the wind. "We're going to save these blossoms tonight, Annie. That's why I'm here."

"Thanks, Brett." She smiled grimly. "I appreciate every hand." As she got into her jeep and led the way back to the house, Annie concluded that Brett Meyer might not consider himself a hero, but he certainly sounded like one to her. He was here to save her precious crop, come hell or a killing frost, even if it took all night. She liked his positive attitude. And she certainly needed his help.

Maybe this was what Aunt Annalee had been trying to tell her at the mission: that she would have the help she needed. Or that help would arrive in the form of a very attractive hero who happened to be a neighbor. She decided she'd better not discuss her theory about Aunt Annalee communicating with her; everyone would think she'd flipped her wig. Everyone but Diego.

Brett followed Annie's old, repainted red-and-white Jeep. He hadn't even been back home two hours, he mused, and here he was fighting the elements again. How well he remembered the years when he'd helped his dad in the struggle against nature, trying to survive on the ranch. The struggle was never ending. And sometimes impossible to win.

The futility of battling nature, coupled with the desire for more control over his life, had driven Brett away from the ranch. Ironically, on the streets of Miami, he had engaged in what seemed an equally futile struggle. And in the end, as his life hung by a thread for days, the only control he had was in exercising a strong will to live.

So here he was again, come full circle, back to the land and nature. At least, hauling smudge pots wasn't life threatening, he thought ruefully, though this was not exactly how he had envisioned spending his recuperation time. Relaxing in a hammock poolside was more what he had in mind. But his dad had said he was needed on the ranch. Brett had been shocked by how run-down the old homestead was. And now, with a frost in late April, Annie needed him, too.

He hadn't expected much when he returned home; he certainly hadn't expected Annie Clayton. So far, she was the only bright spot on his horizon. He figured that fighting to save her apple crop might not be such a bad way to spend his first night, after all. It sure beat staring at the chipped paint on the walls of the old ranch house.

When they arrived at Annie's house, Diego was pulling up in his ancient pickup. Brett remembered the truck from his younger days when he used to hitch a ride into town with his neighbor, thinking it was a miracle it still ran. For a moment, he was overcome by a wave of nostalgia and the warm feelings that swept over him when he glimpsed Diego.

The old man began slowly climbing out of the truck, and then he spotted Brett. With a big, toothless smile lighting up his darkly tanned face, he moved a little quicker.

With a shout, Brett stepped forward to shake Diego's hand and hug him at the same time. "How are you? You're looking fine for a farmer!"

"You're looking pretty fine, yourself, Mr. FBI Big Shot!"

"Nothing like putting me in my place, Diego. And big shot is right! Want to see my scars?"

"Want to see mine?" Diego countered. "I was in the big war and took a couple of bullets. But I didn't get to lay around in the hospital for months."

"Look, you two," Annie interrupted with a chuckle. "We'll have show-and-tell another time. Right now, Brett's offered to help, and we need to take advantage, before he changes his mind."

"When he sees what hard work this is, he might call the FBI and beg them to take him back!" Diego chortled.

"That fancy desk might look pretty good to you after tonight, Brett," she agreed.

He shook his head. "Never. I'd much rather be on my feet and busy."

Annie touched his arm and murmured seriously, "Look, if there's some work you can't do, because of your injuries, just say so. We'll handle the heavy stuff."

"I can handle anything," he said with bravado. "I'm fine."

She could tell she'd struck a nerve with this proud man. "Okay, you asked for it. Diego, show him where we keep the smokers and help him load the rest of them in his truck. Then you two can finish distributing them around the perimeter. Okay?"

"*Sí, señorita.*" Diego grinned up at Brett. "I never thought I'd see you show up to save a crop of apples. Throw them, maybe. But not save them."

"Don't you think I should somehow pay for all those apples I ate?" Brett clapped his hand on Diego's shoulder.

"All the apples you *stole*, you mean!" Diego shook a wrinkled brown finger at Brett.

Annie smiled at the warm banter between the two men. She supposed in all the years Diego had spent here, he had quite a few memories of the rascally kid who had lived next door. Apparently Brett remembered the relationship fondly, too.

They were heading for the shed when a large suburban vehicle pulled in behind the sheriff's truck. With a little cry of joy, Annie ran to greet the occupants.

"Lacy!" She hugged the vivacious redhead who hopped out first. "Am I glad to see you! All of you," she added as a man and two teenaged boys joined them.

"Who said you can't do anything about the weather?" Lacy asked. "I brought my own army to fight the killer frost. And I see the sheriff's here."

"No, the sheriff's son," Annie said in a low voice.

"Ah, the hero." Lacy gave her a knowing smile. "I've been looking forward to meeting him."

"Come on." Annie motioned to Lacy's little army. "Brett Meyer, I want you to meet Silverton's mayor, Lacy Donahue—no, it's Henderson now. And her husband, Holt." She mumbled apologetically, "Sorry about that slip."

Holt stepped forward to shake Brett's hand. "Nice to meet you, Brett. This is our foster son, Roman Barros. And our friend, Steve Amado."

Steve stared in awe at the man who had made the news in such a spectacular way.

"Yo, man." Roman was less intimidated. He regarded Brett curiously. "I've never met an FBI agent before."

"You didn't expect horns, did you?" Brett laughed and shook their hands.

"I read about you in the paper. They called you a real hero." Roman was obviously impressed with the man who shared his Hispanic heritage and had reached such status. "Hey, I'd like to be a hero if I could drive a slick Mercedes like yours, Mr. Meyer."

Annie raised her eyebrows. No wonder he'd driven his dad's truck today. A Mercedes would be as obvious as his spit-polished boots, only bigger.

Brett grinned sheepishly. "How did you know about the car, Roman?"

"A fancy car like that can't slip into this town without somebody knowing it!"

"Actually, there aren't many cars of any kind that slip into this town without Roman knowing it," Holt said with a wry smile. Then he gestured toward his small crew. "We're ready to work, Annie. Just tell us what to do. None of us have any experience with apples."

"First, the rest of the smudge pots have to be placed around the orchards. Leave the chimneys and fuel lines open. Then they need to be filled with fuel. Diego can show you how that's done."

"Okay, you guys hit the orchards," Lacy said. "I'll get supper started. Come on, Annie. Help me with the groceries." She lifted the huge coffeepot and thrust it into Annie's waiting arms. "Sandy sent this. Makes thirty cups."

"That ought to keep us awake for a while." Annie shed her muddy boots on the back porch before entering the kitchen. "What did you bring to eat, Lacy?"

Lacy pulled out a loaf of wheat bread. "Tuna for sandwiches."

"Oh, good. That'll go with the *pozole* I made earlier. What do you need? A big bowl and . . ."

Lacy lined up several items on the counter. "A can opener and a spoon. I brought everything for tuna salad à la Holt. I prefer mine with chives and lemon juice. But he and the kids like sweet pickles and mayo." She wrinkled her nose at Annie.

"In spite of making tuna à la Holt, you seem to be very happy, Lacy."

"I am." Lacy smiled at her old friend.

"But you've got all those kids. There's Roman and his sister and Holt's little girl...." Annie began filling the big coffeepot. "You stepped into a big family. How's it working out?"

"I have lots of help, especially from Mrs. Carson. She's keeping the girls tonight. Everyone pitches in to do their share, and we function as any other family of five. Busy!"

"Sounds like you have everything under control, though." Annie plugged in the coffeepot.

"We aren't perfect. What family is? The important thing is that we're a real family. And the kids are thriving on it." Lacy grinned as she stirred the huge bowl of tuna salad. "So are Holt and I."

Annie handed Lacy a tray for the sandwiches. "You're so lucky to have found a man like Holt." She thought of her own bitter experience with a man she'd thought she loved, and sighed. "Ah, the coffee smells great."

Lacy began piling her sandwiches onto the tray. "Know what would be good with the coffee? Some of your fabulous apple bread."

Annie set out paper plates and napkins. "I knew you liked it, so I took some out of the freezer." She surveyed the kitchen. "Now, where the heck is the other one? I could swear I took three loaves of apple bread out of the freezer today and left them on the counter to thaw. But there are only two here."

"You must be mistaken."

"Obviously I am." Annie checked the freezer. There was a large empty space, big enough for three loaves. She *had* gotten three loaves; she was sure of it. But there was too much to do to waste time worrying about a loaf of apple bread.

She lifted the lid of the huge pot on the stove, intending to stir the *pozole*, a Mexican stew made from lean pork and fresh hominy. Annie spiced hers with ground red chili. She stared in dismay at the pot. "It . . . it's half gone. I *know* I made more than this, Lacy. The pot was so full, I could hardly stir it."

Lacy peered into the half-empty pot. "Maybe it boiled down."

"Hominy doesn't boil down. It swells."

"Well, someone came in and ate some. Diego?"

"Must be." Annie placed the lid on the two-gallon pot. "But I can't imagine when he did it. He's been so busy all afternoon."

Lacy gestured at the pot. "Obviously he found time."

Annie shrugged. "I'm going to relieve the men so they can come in and eat. Are you ready for them?"

"Send in the hungry hordes! They haven't eaten since lunch." Lacy flourished her spoon.

Annie pulled on her jacket. "I'm so glad you came, Lacy. Thanks. This is almost fun."

"Hey, we can't let you lose this crop, Annie. It's bad for the city's economy."

"Not to mention mine!" Annie scrounged in the hall closet for her gloves, wondering why she was protecting her hands now. Maybe so her hands would be soft for Brett Meyer? A small voice in her head answered, *Yes, why not?* She flung open the back door, calling, "See you later, Lacy."

As she fumbled with her boots on the back porch, she heard a noise and paused to listen. Thinking maybe one of the kids had returned to eat, she looked around, but no one was there. Shrugging, she strode rapidly to her Jeep.

Annie found them at the far corner of the Granny Smith orchard. "You men must be starved. Take my Jeep back to the house. Lacy's ready with sandwiches, coffee and *pozole*."

"Sounds great," Holt said. "I guarantee these fellows are hungry. You didn't let her put chives in the tuna, did you?"

"Sweet pickles. No chives."

"All right! Come on, men. That's our kind of food."

The two boys followed him eagerly.

Annie climbed into the truck bed and began pushing another smudge pot toward the rear. "Diego, you and Brett should go eat, too."

"You go on, Diego. I'll help Annie with these." Brett grabbed the pot she had scooted to the edge and hefted it easily. "Eating will keep you warm on a night like this."

"*Sí, sí,* I'm starved. Haven't eaten all afternoon. Anyway, Annie's *pozole* is God's food."

"Come on, Diego, I know you tried it," Annie teased. "It isn't too hot and spicy, is it?"

"*No sé, señorita.* I don't know." He limped toward the Jeep.

"Diego, you didn't have any *pozole*?" she called after him. "Just a little bit?"

"No time today, *señorita.*"

She was confused. If Diego hadn't helped himself, then who? "Hope you enjoy it," she called. "Stay long enough to get warm, now." She stood in the truck bed and watched the Jeep disappear in the growing darkness.

Maybe she had been wrong about the missing food. Maybe she'd been so busy she had misjudged the quantity.

"Are you there, Annie?" Brett asked, breaking into her thoughts.

"Huh? Oh, sure." She hunkered down beside the remaining heaters. "Go ahead and drive to the next drop-off spot."

They worked diligently for the next hour, then joined the others for hot food and to wait for the inevitable temperature drop. Around midnight, Lacy and Holt took the boys home. Diego dozed on the roll-away bed in the laundry room, just off the kitchen. Annie and Brett were left alone in the vigil. They lingered over one more cup of coffee.

"You have some very nice friends." Brett circled his cup with one large hand, drinking from it as if it were a glass.

"They're terrific," Annie agreed.

"Now, how the heck did Roman see my car? I just drove through town and straight out here."

"That's all he needed." She narrowed her eyes. "Personally, I think he has a spy network in town."

"Amazing." Brett shook his head and finished his cup of coffee. "I'm impressed with what's been happening in Silverton since the smelter closed. I'd figured that would spell the end of an era and a town."

"You don't know our mayor. And the townspeople. Everybody's been working awfully hard to make it a viable place to live."

"But there's still no nightlife." Brett leaned back and rubbed his neck.

"No. I guess we're too busy keeping things going in the daytime to worry about nights."

"You like it here, Annie?"

"Yes." She grinned. "Even without a nightlife."

"Then you must be used to . . . ah, small-town living."

"I am now, but before I moved here two years ago I lived in San Francisco. So I've had my share of fast living."

He raised his eyebrows. "And you didn't find the adjustment difficult?"

"Honestly, I've been too busy to notice." She refilled their cups. "When I first came here it was to take care of my terminally ill aunt. Then last year, Uncle Martin died and left me to run the whole farm. Believe me, it was a tremendous mess. He'd neglected it for years while Aunt Annalee was sick. We haven't had a profitable crop in about five seasons. That's why this one is so important—I just don't have the money to carry it any longer."

"What did you do in San Francisco?"

"I was in banking and finance."

"Sounds like a pretty lucrative job."

"I was making more money than I am here," she admitted.

"Then, why did you leave?"

She fiddled with her cup handle. "This probably isn't a good night to explain, but I like the challenges here. Of course, this freezing weather is a little too much. But out here, you have to take what comes. The physical part of the work is rewarding."

He picked up her hand and balanced it in his palm. "Is it worth this?" With the lightest touch she'd ever felt, he stroked the wind-roughened top of her hand, then turned it over to reveal a couple of old blisters. He pressed the center of her palm with two fingers, and she felt the soft caress throughout her entire body.

"I think so." Her voice was tight, and she swallowed hard to relieve the tension in her throat. "It's serene here."

"Serene? Isn't that another word for boring?"

"Maybe. It probably wouldn't satisfy someone who wanted a faster paced life-style."

"I think . . ." He closed his other hand over hers, sandwiching it between his warm palms. "I think I'd like to go to San Francisco with you, Annie. We could have a good time together."

"Probably." Her heart was pounding so wildly inside her breast, she wondered if he could hear it.

"Maybe I could persuade you to go with me sometime."

"And ride in your slick Mercedes?" She smiled faintly, somehow not able to imagine herself in such a fancy car. She was more the four-wheel-drive type. As much as she liked Brett, she had to admit they were quite different. Her muddy boots contrasted with his shiny ones. Her rough hands clashing with his smooth ones.

"You'd look mighty fine in that car, Annie. With your hair blowing in the wind." His gaze swept over her tousled curls, and he smiled. "Yes, yes, I can see it now. A big smile on your face and those beautiful green eyes shining."

She refused to be drawn into his fantasy; it wasn't hers. "I . . . I can't picture it, Brett. I guess I'm too down-to-earth."

"How long has it been since you've been out of town, Annie?"

"Too long, I guess."

"I'd say so."

"I think we'd better put fantasies aside." Reluctantly she brought them back to the cold reality of their vigil. "It's time to check the temperature."

He stood and pulled her to her feet, still holding her hand. "Be sure and get your gloves. It's real cold out there."

As they were ready to leave, she gave him a warm smile. "I do appreciate your help tonight, Brett."

He reached for his jacket, and she noted how powerful his upper arms and shoulders looked. "What are neighbors for?"

"You're a good one. And I'm going to return this favor as soon as I can. I'm a whiz at house painting."

He shrugged broad shoulders into his jacket. "I doubt if you'll have to bother, Annie. I probably won't be here that long. I'm afraid this isn't the place for me."

She felt as though he'd struck her. *Won't be here long?* Where had she gotten the idea that he was here to stay? From him? Or J.M.? Or was it her own private little wish? The brief time she'd spent with him had had her imagining that something might develop between them.

She should have remembered that Brett Meyer was no longer a rancher. Now he was a worldly man, commended for being injured in the line of duty, someone accustomed to more excitement than firing smudge pots around a bunch of apple trees. She couldn't expect him to be satisfied with a quiet place like Silverton. Or with someone like her, seeking independence and serenity.

Annie followed Brett to his father's truck, their breaths making frosty white puffs in the frigid air. Well, she decided, the best she could say about Sheriff Meyer's hero-son was that he was a hard worker. And she'd gotten her hopes up for nothing.

2

ANNIE DRIFTED TO SLEEP around five in the morning. They had fought their battle with Mother Nature and there was nothing more to do but wait. She had no patience for waiting.

Brett, on the other hand, had no trouble staying awake. He had done this a thousand times on surveillance missions, with much less interesting subjects to focus on than Annie Clayton. He felt a little like a voyeur, taking such pleasure in watching her sleep. Nevertheless, he couldn't take his eyes off Annie.

She had been such a surprise, such a refreshing delight to find in a place he thought was devoid of pleasures. Her natural beauty took on an innocent quality in her slumber. And innocence was something he'd found lacking in his world.

After ten years in the business of catching criminals, Brett, who'd started out with idealistic notions, was cynical and bitter. The women he encountered were hard and streetwise. Even the nice ones were recovering from something . . . drugs, alcohol, abuse, rejection.

But Annie was refreshingly different, and he was definitely attracted to her. Besides, she was a stable, practical woman who didn't shirk her duties, belying the fact that she looked delicate and fragile, like someone who couldn't quite handle it all.

He became intrigued by the sweetheart curve of her mouth. Right now, her lips were relaxed and soft and slightly parted—positively sensuous. In contrast, her hands were red-blotched and blistered, her nails short and unglamorous. One hand cradled her face as she slumped on the sofa pillow, the other lay palm up and gently curved on her thigh. In spite of their flaws, they were pretty hands, hardworking hands, and he imagined what it would be like to hold them, to feel their caress.

With a low moan, he pushed himself upright in the chair and stretched. One hand went automatically to his rib cage, and he softly rubbed the scar below the last rib. It ached, and he felt very tired.

Before the injury, a night like this would have been no effort. He could have done anything—lift, run, lose sleep, pick up a few hours in a catnap here or there— nothing bothered him. As a man in excellent physical condition, Brett had always bounced back easily.

Now every exertion or change of pace sapped his energy and made him feel like hell for days. Maybe the agency had been right to pull him off the streets. He simply wasn't up to it anymore, although he would never admit that to anyone. What he needed was time to recuperate, which was why he'd come here.

He gazed at Annie. What he needed was . . . a good woman. Someone attractive and fun. Someone to bring a little laughter to his life. Perhaps someone like Annie.

Instinct told him, though, that Annie was not the type of woman who would go for a fling. And he wanted nothing more right now.

With effort, he pushed himself to his feet. Slowly he straightened, his body aching. Damn, he hated what the injury had done to him, how it had changed his life. He ambled into the kitchen and fixed a pot of coffee. While the coffee sputtered through the drip system, he stepped to the back porch and checked the thermometer. She'd want to know. Then he walked over to where Annie lay sleeping and reached out to her. It was time.

Annie felt something nudge her shoulder. A low, masculine voice rumbled her name. "Annie, Annie."

She fought the heavy sleep that tried to hold her. "Huh?" Through her haze she saw a darkly handsome face with intelligent ebony eyes and a thin, noble nose. She blinked several times. "Brett?"

"It's morning. Want to check your blossoms?"

"Oh. Yes." She tried to focus, to force herself awake. Sitting up, she pushed her thick mane of hair back. "What time is it?"

"After nine."

"What's the temp?"

"Thirty on the back porch." He walked toward the kitchen. "Coffee?"

"Hmm. Is it ready?" She followed him, rubbing her eyes and trying to straighten her hair with her hands. "I must look awful."

He noted the wild disarray of her hair and gave her a wry smile. "Where I come from, that's the style."

"Out here, style doesn't matter." She gazed out the window over the sink. "Now that the sun's up, we can close down the smokers."

"Right. I'll help you." He handed her a steaming mug of coffee.

She was encouraged by the sight of the sun glistening on the white-blossomed trees. They didn't look brown, at least not from here. "The damage is done, you know. It's over. They either made it, or they didn't."

"I know." Those statements could apply to him as well as to the apple blossoms, he thought. The damage was done to him—to his career. Even though he hadn't intended to hang around here very long, maybe he should unpack, after all.

Annie bent over the cup and inhaled the coffee's aroma. "Ahhh, smells good." She turned an innocent, fresh-morning smile on him. "This is very nice of you, Brett, to stay and even fix coffee. What would you charge to do this every day? I love waking up to coffee."

He grinned, thinking devilishly that a night spent in the lovely redhead's bed would do it. "I come cheap enough."

"Cheap enough for a farm girl?"

"Depends," he responded, knowing already that Annie was the wrong woman for what he had in mind. He wrapped his fingers around the cup's base, ignoring the handle, and drank his coffee.

She smiled grimly at him. "I'm really very nervous about the blossoms. I'd like to check them now."

"Of course." He could see that she was trying to cover up her uneasiness. Setting his cup onto the counter, he helped her into her jacket.

She paused. "I'm glad you're here, Brett."

He nodded. The sight of the tension around her mouth and the fragile look in her verdant eyes caused an uneasy tightening in his stomach. He realized then that he had to watch himself, or this woman could easily get to him. And he couldn't let that happen, not when he wasn't intending to stay around.

Brett grabbed the door and pushed gently on her shoulder to steer her out. What he really wanted to do was shove her away for a moment so he could draw a clear breath, for he felt overwhelmed by her presence. But he couldn't avoid her; Annie was definitely *there*.

Within minutes, they were lurching along in the truck, heading for the orchards. Annie sat on the edge of the seat and motioned for him to stop at the first row of trees. She bounded out and ran to them with the eagerness of a child at Christmas. Brett followed her at a slower pace, reminded by his aching body that he wasn't young and invincible anymore.

The hopefulness in her face vanished; her shoulders drooped. "Some of these were hit. See? They're already turning brown."

Brett stood beside her, examining the tree full of blossoms. He walked to the inside row. "Not all of them, Annie. Some made it. These are in better shape. That's the first row to be hit by the cold air as it comes across the valley."

"You're right. Let's spot-check all the way up to the mission ruins." She closed the still-smoking chimney of the nearby smudge pot and headed for the truck.

They drove the narrow roads between the small orchards of Granny Smiths and Rome Beauties, stopping occasionally to evaluate the blossoms and shut the chimney valves on the pots.

When they reached the mission, at the far end of the last orchard, Annie was encouraged. "They look better here. I don't see any brown ones!" She ran from tree to tree. "These are in very good shape, Brett! I don't think I lost many up here at all!"

He followed her, closing chimneys as he went. "They're protected by the mission walls."

She halted and looked at him. "The mission protected my blossoms?" Her gaze flew to the crumbling bricks of the ancient facade.

"Sure. The structure probably took the full brunt of the wind. Also, it's higher here. The cold air naturally drains down the slope."

Annie's voice held a touch of awe. "I know this sounds strange, but sometimes I feel that this place is special. Like now."

"Well, there is something to be said for a building that's lasted so long. What is it, a hundred fifty, two hundred years old?"

"Not just that. Sometimes I think that someone watches over things from here."

He raised his eyebrows. "Like who?"

"I don't know, but . . . it isn't unusual for people to feel strange or . . . or even to hear things when they're out here. My dog, Feliz, won't come around it. She stays in the Jeep when I bring her out here."

"So?"

"Sometimes animals sense things." Annie could see the skepticism in Brett's dark eyes, but it suddenly seemed important for him to understand. "Uncle Martin didn't like having this old mission here and wanted to tear it down. But Aunt Annalee intervened. She said this was a sacred place and should be left alone."

"Are you saying that *you* feel strange when you come here, Annie?"

"Oh, no. I like it." She grinned. "But sometimes I hear things. Like voices." She knew she was pushing her credibility with him.

"You hear people's voices?"

"Sometimes." She hurried to qualify her statement. "Oh, not just anybody. Someone very close to me. My aunt, usually."

"You think Aunt Annalee speaks to you?" There was a growing degree of incredulity in his voice.

"She...her spirit seems very strong to me when I come here. Diego says *los espíritus* who have gone before us live here. That their eyes, *los ojos*, watch us." She made a nervous little laugh. "You don't believe this, do you?"

"In ghosts? No." His tone was definite.

Annie figured that now was not the time to tell him about her strange vibes from Aunt Annalee only two days ago when she related that someone was coming to help on the farm. And now, Annie felt that Aunt Annalee was referring to *him*. No. She was already pushing credibility with Brett. "But you must admit, there are some things that defy explanation."

"There's an answer to everything somewhere."

"Maybe so. But we can't know everything." She smiled sweetly, unwilling to concede her private beliefs, weird though they might be. "You don't feel *los ojos* watching us right now, even though we're supposed to be alone?"

"Do you?"

She looked back at the mission. "Uh-huh. I feel...*something*."

"No, I don't feel eyes watching us," he said definitely, rocking back on his heels and eyeing her with skepticism. "Look, Annie, no one is going to finish this job for us. So why don't we forget this supernatural voices-in-the-mission nonsense and get on with our business?"

Annie agreed, thinking she had pressed the conservative-thinking Mr. Meyer far enough. She went down each row, moving from one glowing chimney to another. When she reached the end of the row, she noticed that a pot was missing where one should have been placed. She quickly dismissed it. Now was not the time to further speculate on vanishing items. They had a big job to finish.

Climbing back into the truck, they drove past the mission, heading for another section.

"Wait!" Annie grabbed Brett's arm. "There it is!"

"What?"

She pointed. Beside the mission's crumbling corner was a smudge pot, glowing and apparently still lit. "The pot! One was missing from my row, and there it is."

They got out of the truck and approached the still-warm smoker. "Now, how do you explain that?" she challenged.

"Must be one of your ghosts," he scoffed. Reaching up with his heavily gloved hand, he closed the chimney. "I'd be willing to bet that if you questioned those kids who were here last night, you'd find the culprit."

"Hmm." She nodded. "Okay, logic wins." She followed Brett back to the truck. She'd forgotten she was talking to a former arm of the law. He could probably draw the truth from those dry adobe walls of that two-hundred-year-old mission. And he would never believe a poltergeist moved that heavy smoker.

She didn't, either. Not really. But it was fun to speculate.

NIGHT COULDN'T COME soon enough for Annie. Assured by the local weather report that there was no chance of another spell of freezing weather, she took a hot bath and donned her favorite long flannel gown. The forecast called for rain.

As she slid between the sheets, she could hear the promised rain sporadically hitting the roof. Soon the drops fell in a relaxing patter, and she began to drift.

Her rambling thoughts strayed to her new neighbor. Ruggedly handsome with his dark skin and hair and those devastating ebony eyes, he had an aura about him that made its way into her fantasy.

In his maturity, Brett had acquired a lean, muscular body that attracted her in a purely sensuous way. He wasn't the skinny kid next door anymore, but an experienced, if somewhat jaded, man with an intriguing past. That he had integrity was obvious from his actions: he'd come to help her and remained through the time of crisis. He had even stayed to help her close the chimneys, a time-consuming job, but one that she and Diego could have handled.

Still, part of her wanted to believe that he hadn't simply stayed out of a sense of duty, but because he had wanted to be there.

Even in her semidream state, though, Annie knew it was folly to think Brett wanted to be with her specifically. The man didn't want to be back in Silverton at all, and he wouldn't be staying long. The sooner she accepted that fact, the better off she would be.

Between her exhaustion and the rhythmic patter of the rain, Annie willingly succumbed to the glorious sleep that claimed her. In her final moments of consciousness, she heard someone speaking softly, fluidly in Spanish. It sounded like Diego and…a woman…. She fell asleep before she had a chance to wonder about the woman.

A CRASH WOKE HER. Glass breaking. Then, dead silence.

She wasn't sure how long she had been asleep, but the room was pitch-black. It was still night. Her heart pounded, pumping adrenaline throughout her body, waking her completely and quickly. The sound had come from her bathroom.

Her first thought was that a rat or a raccoon had gotten inside the house. She'd had problems with both creatures, and her constant fear was that one would invade her home. Cautiously she slid from the bed. Just to be on the safe side, she grabbed the first weapon available, a small stick of wooden molding used to prop the window open.

She stalked to the door, then paused to listen. The shower curtain rustled against the tub. Slipping her hand around the door facing, she switched on the light. The small room appeared empty. The shower curtain hanging above the tub moved slightly.

Aha! She stepped inside, using her stick to push aside the curtain. She took another quick step to see the culprit, and an acute pain stabbed her foot.

"Ouch! What the—" Annie drew back against the wall and grabbed her foot. In her haste, she'd forgotten about the crash that had awakened her, and what had obviously caused it. Unthinkingly she had stepped barefoot into the broken glass on the hard tile floor. She stared at the slash on her foot and the blood that gushed from her instep and dripped to the floor. "Oh, no!"

As she reached for a towel, Annie caught sight of two brown eyes peering out from behind the curtain. Then, a face. But this wasn't a creature. This was a girl. A very scared girl.

Feeling absolutely no fear, Annie dropped her stick and wrapped the towel around her foot to stop the bleeding. She was more angry than scared at her intruder. "See what you did!"

The girl surprised her by speaking English. "I am sorry."

"Sorry I woke up? Or sorry you dropped this uh . . ." Annie examined the mess on the floor. "This peroxide bottle?"

"I did not intend to drop it."

"I bet not!" Annie squeezed her foot. "You didn't intend to wake me, so you could take whatever you wanted."

The girl stared silently at Annie, her large brown eyes wide with fright. An elegant blue silk *rebozo*, a traditional shawl worn by Hispanic women, draped her dark hair and shoulders. It was spotted from the rain. Her colorfully embroidered dress was elaborately handmade. She was barefoot.

"What are you doing in here, anyway?"

The girl looked down. Annie noticed that she was shivering.

"What do you want?"

Still crouched in the tub, the girl shrugged slim shoulders. There was an intangible something about her that seemed almost regal, and bespoke fine breeding.

"You came here to steal from me, didn't you?" Annie demanded.

"No." The girl lifted her head proudly.

"Then, what? Why else would you slip in here in the middle of the night?"

"I needed—" the girl pointed to the broken bottle "—that."

"Peroxide? For what?"

"Medicine. *Por favor*, just give me some medicine, and let me leave. I promise I will not bother you again. I will go away, far away." The girl gestured with one hand.

Annie was struck by the gracefulness of the motion, like the sweep of a dancer's arm. "First you have to clean up this mess you made. Then we'll talk about giving you medicine."

"*Sí, gracias.*" The girl stepped gingerly out of the tub. Soon she had the broken glass scooped into the rubber wastebasket and was soaking up the spilled peroxide with a towel.

Annie found some alcohol under the sink and a box of bandages. She sat on the toilet seat and examined the inch-long cut on her foot. For such a little slit, she observed, it certainly bled a lot. Maybe she could avoid having stitches by pulling the bandage tight. Gritting her teeth, Annie splashed the cut with antiseptic. She moaned as the stinging ran through her foot.

Calmly the girl took over from Annie, wiping around the wound with gentle hands, making sure there were no glass shards, then closing it tightly with a bandage. When she was finished, she looked to Annie for approval.

Annie. "Thank you. That's a pretty good job. I couldn't have done better, myself."

The girl clutched the box of bandages and the alcohol bottle to her breast. "Can I have these, *por favor*?"

"Why do you need them? Are you injured?"

"No, not for me. For..." The girl hesitated, her eyes cast downward. "For someone else."

"Is that person injured badly? Does he or she need help?"

"No, no! This is enough."

"You don't want me to know about your business, do you?"

"*No, señorita.*" The girl's tone was apologetic but firm. "This is all I need. Thank you. I will go now. Far away." The girl clutched the items and started backing out of the bathroom as if afraid Annie would change her mind.

Annie made no attempt to stop her, even though she wanted to. "Thank you for fixing my foot."

"Do not thank me for cutting you. I am sorry for that." The girl's English was halting but understandable. "Please, forgive me." She turned and fled the room.

Annie hobbled after her.

In the hallway, she ran into Diego, who prevented her from following the girl. "Diego! Get out of my way! Stop that girl!"

"She is gone, *señorita*."

Annie wrested herself from his arms and switched on the kitchen light. "Diego, what are you doing here?" He slept in a little room that adjoined the shed out back. Only occasionally, did he sleep in the laundry room as he had last night during the freeze.

"I heard noises."

She folded her arms. "What's going on here, Diego? I heard you talking to someone earlier. Was it her?"

His shoulders slumped. He was obviously unwilling to lie to Annie. *"Sí,"* he said finally. "I tried to keep her from entering the house. But she insisted."

"She claimed she needed medicine, Diego."

"Sí. Es verdad. The truth."

"Is someone hurt?"

"I don't know."

"You *do* know!"

He shuffled around a little. "It is the old woman. Something is wrong with her leg. She needs medicine."

"An old woman is with this girl? Is she sick?"

"I . . . I think so."

"Where are they?"

"I don't know."

"You do."

"I cannot tell. Please don't make me. They will leave, now that they've been discovered."

"How many are there?"

"Just the two."

"Only two women? Alone?"

"Sí."

"That's strange." Annie pondered the situation a moment. In her experience, women didn't ordinarily travel alone like that. But, this wasn't an ordinary situation, obviously.

"Where are they staying?"

He shook his head and looked down at his feet.

"Where, Diego?" she demanded. "Where are those women hiding? The ruins?"

His affirmative nod was almost imperceptible.

She pretended not to react to the knowledge that they were in such a special place, but inside she raged. How dare they invade her private sanctum? "Do you think this medicine is enough? It's only alcohol. Not very strong."

"*Sí*. It will be enough."

"Maybe she needs a doctor—"

"No! No, I do not think so."

Annie looked steadily at him. "They're illegals, aren't they, Diego?"

He studied his shoes, finally mumbling, "*Sí, señorita.*"

"I told you before that I don't hire illegals. It's against the law, and I don't do it."

"I know. They will leave."

"They have to be gone tomorrow, Diego. Off my property. See to it." She motioned toward the door. "Now, you go on back to bed. I'm going to try to get some sleep in what's left of this miserable night."

Annie locked the back door, switched off the kitchen light and hobbled back to her bedroom. As she settled into the warm, dry cocoon of her bed, she wondered where the girl and the old woman were bedding down. And if they were dry on such a rainy night. Maybe Diego had given them some kind of shelter and that was why he was so jumpy.

She tried to put the night's disruption out of her mind. It was illegal to hire aliens without green cards. Annie's policy had always been to refuse them when they came looking for work. It was too risky. Anyway, the sheriff owned the next ranch. It wouldn't take him long to find out if she started hiring aliens. Well, she just wouldn't do it, that's all.

Slowly the answers for the unaccountable events of the past few days began to emerge. The noises, the missing apple bread and *pozole*. The misplaced smudge pot at the mission. Even the strange feeling of being watched—suddenly it was all clear to her. They weren't *los espíritus* at the mission. They were illegal aliens. Annie slept restlessly with that knowledge for the remainder of the night.

THE NEXT MORNING about ten o'clock she heard a car and looked out to see Brett parking his sleek silver-gray Mercedes next to her decrepit Jeep. Roman was right. That car was extremely noticeable.

However grand the car seemed, though, it was no more impressive than the man who climbed out and made his way through the mud to her house.

She pushed open the door with an eagerness she couldn't help. "Come on in, Brett. Want some coffee?"

He scraped his shiny black boots on the welcome mat before stepping inside. "Sure." The warm fragrance of apples greeted him and brought a smile. "Coffee sounds great. I'm doing a little business for my dad today, Annie. He's been notified of a dozen or so illegal aliens from Nicaragua. They were supposed to be met by sanctuary workers and trucked northward. He wants everyone, especially in outlying areas like this, to keep an eye out for them."

Annie felt a tightening in her chest. "Thanks for the warning." She hobbled around the kitchen, busying herself with warming two slices of apple bread.

"Annie! What happened to your foot?"

"I, uh, oh, just . . . cut it on some glass. That's one of the problems with these clay tile floors. Every darn thing that drops on them breaks instantly. It's nothing but an inconvenience." She moved clumsily to the table with a plate of apple bread.

She wasn't sure why she didn't simply tell him about the intruder last night. The illegals were gone by now. She owed them nothing, especially not loyalty. They would only be trouble for her, and she would not protect them.

But telling Brett about them would only upset him. He might even do something rash, like call in his father. She certainly didn't want a bunch of uniformed officers stomping around the ruins. Besides they would be long gone by now. Out of sight, out of mind.

"Thanks for helping me during the freeze, Brett." She poured mugs of coffee for them and took a seat opposite him. "I really appreciate all your time and work you gave me."

"Have you assessed your damage?"

"Thanks to you and everyone who helped, it's in the hundreds of dollars, not thousands."

"Then you won't lose your entire crop?"

"No, thank goodness."

"If the farm went under, would you have to return to San Francisco?"

She shrugged. "I'd probably have to if I wanted to get a job."

He grinned devilishly. "Then I defeated my own purpose. My intent to get you to San Francisco was foiled by my efforts to save your apple crop here."

She stiffened with indignation. "Can't you understand, Brett? This is where I want to be." She tapped the tabletop for emphasis. "Where I want to stay."

"Too bad. We could have had such fun traveling."

"I have work to do." She shook her head. "No time to play."

"Then the only way I'll get to see you is to work with you?"

"Looks that way."

"What's next?"

"I need to get the irrigation system going. We've had a few problems with the sprinklers and pipes in one area. Then I'll put spreaders on the Grannies."

"Those little sticks that you put on the branches to re-shape them?"

"Right. They help spread the branches out so the sun-light can get to them better."

"Can I help?"

She shrugged, feigning nonchalance. "If you're going to be here long enough."

"I'll be here," he admitted shortly.

Annie smiled, feeling a sense of elation at the news. "You're a good neighbor to have, Brett. I hope you stay a while."

"I'd rather be your good friend than just a good neigh-bor, Annie." And he'd rather they were good lovers than anything else, but he knew he couldn't say that.

"You are," she said warmly, meaning it sincerely.

They chatted about inconsequential things while they finished the apple bread and coffee. Brett found himself lingering, reluctant to leave the relaxed setting and the company of this woman. But he had an obligation to his dad, and Annie had work to do. He shoved his chair back. "I'd better be going. Be sure to watch for any strangers. Call the sheriff's office right away if you have any problems. Or send Diego over to the ranch for me."

"Right." After the strained conversation with Diego last night, the idea of sending him for Brett's help in the matter seemed ludicrous.

"I'm getting a phone installed at the house tomorrow, so you can call me if you need anything."

She grinned. "People only have phones installed if they're going to be in town a while."

"I'll be there at least long enough to get the first month's bill."

A month. Okay. She waved as he disappeared into his Mercedes. A snazzy car for a noble man with shiny boots and a dazzling smile.

As soon as Brett left, Diego hurried breathlessly into the kitchen and confronted Annie. "Please, you must come. The old woman is very sick. She needs . . . help. You've got to do something, Annie!"

"Diego, you must have heard Brett, since you were waiting out there on the porch. They're looking for illegals now." She folded her arms and gave him a scolding glare. "Diego, tell me the truth. These women aren't from Mexico, are they? They're from Nicaragua."

He gazed at her bleakly. There was no avoiding the truth now. He nodded. *"Sí, señorita."*

She ran her hand beneath her hair and massaged her neck for a long moment. "Oh, great! You know that Brett is FBI. That's *federal* police, Diego! These people are international refugees, hiding on my property! Well, they just have to go, that's all there is to it. They have to go!"

"Sí, señorita." He held his hat anxiously with both hands. "Would you come now to see the old woman?"

She whirled around and glared at him. "Haven't you heard anything I've said? This is against the law! I can't—"

He was steadily persistent. "*Por favor,* she is very sick."

Annie sighed heavily, shaking her head in frustration. He would not take no for an answer. "All right, Diego. I'll see what I can do."

"*Gracias.*"

Even as she climbed into the old truck beside Diego, Annie figured this was one of the craziest, most dangerous, most stupid things she had done since she had exchanged her nice, secure job in San Francisco for the risky apple farm in New Mexico. And yet, she found that she could not refuse to help.

3

ANNIE FELT a little foolish when Diego drove to the mission ruins and stopped beside the misplaced smudge pot.

Here she had imagined her aunt's presence, when it was actually the presence of someone real she'd sensed. Wouldn't Brett Meyer have a good laugh over this, if he ever found out.

Well, she didn't care what he thought. She would still think of Aunt Annalee's spirit dwelling out here. Anyway, Brett would never need to know about these illegal aliens on her property. They would be gone soon, and so would he.

Diego led the way around the crumbling facade to an area of the building that was still intact. Annie ducked her head as she followed him through the low doorway built for people much shorter than she. The room was dark.

In the shadows, she discerned the slender young girl who had broken into the house last night. On a crude bed, an older woman huddled under a blanket.

The girl rushed to Diego, murmuring anxiously in Spanish. Diego answered in a calmer, soothing tone. Annie understood only scraps of the conversation as he reassured the girl that Annie would help and could be trusted.

The emotional scene gripped Annie for a moment. Two women, alone in a foreign country—one of them ill, the other very frightened—forced to depend on and trust absolute strangers. What were they doing here? Why were they leaving their homes? Why were they alone? Where was their family? Were there no men in the traveling party? Where were they going? What were their names?

So many questions ran through her mind, but Annie knew she had to deny this natural curiosity. It was dangerous to know too much. She would do whatever she could to assist them and then send them on their way.

She approached the bed. The woman lay with her eyes closed, clutching her cover. Annie recognized the blanket as one of Diego's. "What's wrong with her?" she asked the girl.

"A fever, I think. She is very hot. She cries out in her sleep."

Tentatively, Annie touched the woman's forehead. "Feels like she has a fever, all right. Where does she hurt?" Annie figured the elderly woman could have the flu or even pneumonia, especially living in an exposed environment like this.

"She injured her leg a few weeks ago. She's been sick ever since."

"Her leg? How bad is it? Can I see the injury?" So that was the reason the girl was after the alcohol last night. Annie gently lifted the blanket and gazed intently at the ugly gash above the woman's ankle. Her whole leg was swollen and obviously badly infected.

"She cut it on a fence," the girl said simply.

Annie didn't ask how. She could imagine these two crawling under barbed wire, and it touched her heart to think about it. "I would recommend that she see a doctor. This is beyond my knowledge and my medicine chest."

"Oh, no!" The girl wrung her hands. "We cannot be seen in public! We were warned."

Annie's tone changed. "Listen, she needs an antibiotics, stronger medicine than what I have." Annie shook her head and looked at the woman, who shivered beneath the thin blanket.

"Please, can't you do something? Diego said you would."

"Oh, he did?" She looked accusingly at the old man, then back at the girl, her thin shoulders draped in the elegantly fringed *rebozo*. The beautiful garment, as well as the women, looked terribly out of place in the shabby surroundings of the mission ruins.

Diego spoke hesitantly. "I know I should have asked you first, Annie."

"You're darn right!" Annie's frustration spilled over as anger, and she lashed out at Diego, then at the girl. "What do you expect from me? This...this is illegal! And you! You're breaking the law by slipping into this country and hiding out. You . . . we *all* could be caught!"

At Annie's tirade, the girl edged closer to the bed. "We did not mean to cause trouble for you."

"Good. Because I have no intention of getting mixed up with people like you. It's too dangerous."

"Yes, I know." The girl looked down at the dirt floor.

Annie's gaze followed. The girl's sandals were mere scraps of leather. Her feet were bare and dirty. Taking a deep breath, she fortified herself for a stronger defense.

"Did you also know that the county sheriff owns the ranch next door? And his son who lives there right now is on leave from the FBI? That's like—" Annie gestured in frustration. "Bigger than the border patrol. What would have happened to you if you'd hidden on *his* property? And tried to steal from him? And what if *he'd* found you instead of *me*?"

"He would probably send us back." The girl lifted her chin. "To our certain death."

"Oh," Annie scoffed, shaking her head. "Don't be so dramatic." She didn't want to believe that these women were fleeing for their lives.

"It is true," the girl said soberly. "Please, can't you help us? And we will be on our way. Just a little help?"

The word *help* hung in Annie's mind. When she had needed help during the frost, her friends had been there. Even Brett, who hardly knew her, had given his able assistance. She was grateful to them all. Now, here were these women, all alone, with no one to help them but her.

She took a deep breath and let it out slowly. Annie's thoughts raced as she tried to figure what to do about the women and their problem. First things first. The older woman needed the professional medical care of a doctor. Annie couldn't bear to send them on their way in this condition. "All right, I'll help. But you must do exactly as I say."

"Yes, yes! Anything!"

"The main point is, *don't get caught*." Annie couldn't believe what she was saying. As a more reasonable thought, she added, "And as soon as she's able, you go. Understand?"

The girl nodded solemnly.

"I'll be back in a little while." Annie walked to the door, then paused and turned around. She didn't know why she asked, but it just seemed the natural thing to do. "What are your names?"

"I am Carmen Allende." The girl said with a proud lilt to her voice. "And this is my mother-in-law, Isabel."

Annie bit her lower lip. That was a mistake, she concluded immediately. I shouldn't have asked their names. Now they weren't nameless beings, belonging somewhere else. They were individuals—Carmen and Isabel—and they were in big trouble. They had a story, and families who were probably worried about them, probably wondering where they were right now. Carmen looked too young to be married, she thought, and then wondered what catastrophe had caused her to be traveling with her mother-in-law.

Again Annie caught herself. Those things didn't matter. Those things were not her concern.

"Okay, Carmen," she said in an officious, clipped tone. "I'll be back as soon as I make some arrangements." Annie walked away rapidly. Every answer brought more questions. And she didn't want to think about them.

THAT AFTERNOON, Annie pulled her truck to a stop beside the back door of a small white frame building on the edge of town. She gave her two passengers an encouraging smile. "It's going to be all right. Dr. Theresa will take care of Isabel and keep your secret." It had taken several phone calls for Annie to discover a physician who could be trusted.

Dr. Theresa Hidalgo came highly recommended. She and her husband, Manny, operated a pharmacy and country grocery store next to a small clinic. The store served as a gathering place for the Hispanic community of Silverton.

Annie and Carmen practically carried Isabel up the steps and into the building. Then Annie waited in the truck alone, hoping no one would see her, and worrying more than she should about Isabel's welfare.

Just as she was beginning to think that she would survive her illicit journey undetected, she heard the sound of boots grinding against gravel as someone walked toward the truck.

She looked around in time to see Brett Meyer heading straight for her. Many anxious thoughts passed through her brain, most of them centered on how to flee.

But, no. She couldn't do that. She had to face him, calmly of course, even though guilt was probably written all over her face.

So she sat there waiting for him with a sick little smile, hoping she looked placid. And praying that Carmen and Isabel wouldn't come out of that back door while Brett was here.

In an inspired move, she switched on the radio. Country music blared from the speaker and helped set the casual mood she wanted to portray. She rolled the window down. "Hey, Brett! Fancy seeing you here, of all places." He looked devastating in his gray suede jacket and tight gray cords. And those boots—still shiny.

Annie realized that she was probably too impressed by the sight of a well-dressed man, but around here she saw so few.

"I could say the same, Annie. How are you feeling?"

"Why, I'm fine."

"Is your foot bothering you?"

"My foot?" She stared at him blankly.

"The one that you cut last night."

"Oh. That one." Annie realized instantly that she had let her perfect excuse for seeing the doctor—her cut foot—slip away. She felt silly forgetting about it, but she'd had more to think about today than her own minor injury. "It's much better, thanks."

He nodded, taking a quick assessment of her. "Then you aren't sick?"

It was a ridiculous conversation, traveling in circles. He obviously wanted to know why she was here. She, in turn, was trying *not* to tell him. But she had to tell him something.

"I brought one of my, uh, workers, to see the doctor," Annie said simply.

"I thought it was too early to hire migrants."

"It is, generally, but, a, uh, couple came through asking for jobs. I figured that they could help Diego with some chores around the farm." She brightened and decided to turn the questioning toward him. "How about you, Brett? Did our all-night vigil to save the trees cause a relapse?"

Brett scoffed. "Not at all. That wasn't anything, compared to some of my exploits."

"That's right. I forget you're the local hero who's used to lots of excitement."

"Hero?" Brett looked away and stuck his hands into his jacket pockets in frustration. "Come on, now, Annie. This hero stuff is embarrassing. I'm just an ordinary guy, stopping by to visit some old friends."

Ordinary? she thought. Hardly! "The Hidalgos are old friends?" She shouldn't be too surprised. The Hispanic couple was only a few years older than she. And Brett, she guessed, was about their age.

"Manny and Theresa are old, old friends. Manny and I went to school together at New Mexico Military Institute. And I was best man at their wedding."

"I didn't realize . . ." Annie's anxiety level rose several notches. Now she had to worry that the so-called trustworthy Dr. Theresa might tell her old buddy about the illegals Annie brought in today.

"I also wanted to warn them about the increased number of illegals in the area. Everyone knows they go to Theresa when they're sick."

Annie blinked. Everyone? She hadn't known until she asked around. But then, dealing with illegals wasn't her normal activity. "Are you asking Dr. Theresa to report them?"

Brett shuffled his feet. "No. I feel that kind of pressure would be an unfair imposition on our friendship. Theresa has to live with herself on that issue."

Annie breathed a sigh of relief. Maybe this tough law-and-order man did have a tiny core of humanity, after all. "Yes, I suppose so." She wondered if she could live with herself. Then she thought of the pitiful sight of Isabel on that ragged bed today and knew she could not have lived with herself if she'd turned her back.

"Believe it or not, the local sheriff's department is concerned about more than the individual who tries to slip into this country illegally. These people are being mistreated by transporters."

"We've had those problems for years, Brett."

"Yes, but it's intensified this spring. Dad and his deputies found a truckload of them last night. They'd been locked up for hours and hadn't eaten in several days. One elderly man had to be hospitalized with a bad heart. The others had to be treated for dehydration."

"Are they all right?"

"Yeah. We were lucky that time. But who knows how many more are hiding?"

Annie shook her head as if she'd never heard of such a thing and glanced anxiously at the office's back door. She prayed they wouldn't come out yet.

"Between cutting your foot and this worker getting sick, I'll bet you haven't done much around the farm today."

"Not much."

"So, could you use some help?"

"Well, sure. But you don't have to do that, Brett."

"I'd like to."

"It's too late to get anything done today. Maybe another time."

"Tomorrow, then. Tonight I'll bring supper, and we can talk. Catch up on old times. Okay?"

"Well..." It sounded appealing, if only she didn't have these women to hide. "I—"

"You aren't expecting company, are you?" His dark eyes explored her face.

"No, of course not." If he only knew the kind of company she had, he would be shocked. But how could she refuse this dark-eyed, handsome man? "Come on over."

He grinned. "Now that's more like it, Annie Clayton. I'll see you later." Turning away, he walked back in the direction from which he'd come.

She felt a quickening of anticipation at the thought of spending time with Brett this evening. But she couldn't help being torn between wanting him to come over and the awful responsibility she felt for the women. What if he should catch them? What lame excuse would she give? What would he do?

She couldn't imagine, but she had a pretty good idea. Brett was law and order; she was a softie. He was a tough ex-FBI agent; she was a simple apple farmer who couldn't forget the two women cast by fate into her care and, unfortunately, couldn't turn her back on their plea for help.

Finally the back door of the doctor's office opened, and Dr. Theresa motioned to Annie. She bounded up the steps and entered the tiny back room. Isabel lay on a small bed with Carmen holding her hand.

Annie's glance went from Isabel to Dr. Theresa. She felt more anxious than she had realized. "How is she?"

"I've given her an antibiotic and a tetanus shot. Her daughter-in-law has instructions on how to care for the wound. She needs rest and care. She's malnourished and near exhaustion."

"Then, she's going to be okay?"

"Yes, in time."

Annie frowned and lowered her voice. "How long before she can leave?"

"Not for a while. She's very ill, Annie. I need to run some more tests on her in a few days when she feels better. But an initial screening showed a very high blood sugar."

"Which means?"

"She may be a diabetic. That's probably why the leg wouldn't heal and why this journey has been so hard on her. She has to take better care of herself."

"Or we do." Annie sighed, not fully aware that she was taking the responsibility for Isabel's well-being. "So what do you suggest?"

"Can you . . . will you be able to do what's necessary to take care of her for a little while?"

Annie looked at the two women, then nodded at Dr. Theresa. "Of course."

"If not, maybe I can find someone else. . . ."

"How long are we talking here, Doctor?"

"A few weeks."

"Weeks?" Annie's face registered her feelings of dismay. She was hoping to get rid of them tomorrow. "Weeks," she said slowly.

"Are you okay with this, Annie?" Dr. Theresa asked. "You seem uncomfortable."

"Can you blame me?"

"Not at all. It isn't something most of us plan on doing. But—" Dr. Theresa's gaze went to Isabel for a brief glance.

"We'll do fine," Annie decided quickly. "If anyone asks, I'll just say they're migrant workers. Anyway, I feel responsible. They were on my property. They found me. I'll keep them until—" Annie shook her head and stuffed her hands into her jacket pockets. "I've never done anything like this before, Dr. Theresa. I don't know how to go about it. I want to help, yet I feel so guilty."

Dr. Theresa patted her arm. "You do what your conscience tells you is right. No one can pass judgment on that."

Annie sighed heavily. "Right now, my conscience says to take them home and feed them."

"Mine says the same thing." Dr. Theresa smiled gently. "Now, I'd like to see Isabel in a few days to run a glucose tolerance, which is a series of blood tests over a three-hour period. I'll see her sooner if she doesn't show improvement. Give me a call any time."

"Okay."

"Just take it a day at a time, Annie. If it's too much for you, call me."

"Thanks." Annie turned to her charges. "Okay, Carmen, Isabel, *vámonos*. Let's go. We have lots to do." And in the back of her mind she was thinking that Brett would be over soon for supper. Now how was she going to juggle them all and keep them apart?

WHEN SHE EXPLAINED Isabel's condition to Diego, he insisted that they move into his room. He would gladly sleep in the barn, he said, where the migrants usually slept. Annie agreed that the women couldn't continue to live in the ruins, yet they had to remain hidden. Maybe Diego's room was the safest place, after all.

Annie hadn't gotten the women completely settled when Brett's Mercedes pulled into her driveway. Before heading out to meet him, Annie pulled Diego aside. "Now, listen to me, Diego. Brett Meyer's here, and he's going to stay for supper. You must make sure those women keep out of sight. I'll put food on the porch for all of you in a little while, probably less than an hour. You just quietly slip up there and get it. Okay?"

"*Sí, señorita,*" he said, reverting to the familiar Spanish.

Annie smoothed her sweater and jeans before walking over to greet Brett. She figured her brain must not have been working when she talked to him this afternoon. Why had she allowed him to come over tonight? But when she saw him again, she knew. He was just too irresistible.

"Hope you're hungry for fried chicken," he said when she drew close, lifting the take-out box for her view.

"Sounds great. I'm hungry for anything." She fell into step with him, suddenly elated that he had insisted on coming. "Starved, in fact. I don't think I've taken time to eat all day."

"Not good." He slipped an arm casually around her back as they walked toward the house. "Let's do something about your nutrition."

"We'll fix some coffee, a salad and a vegetable to go with the chicken," she said eagerly, forgetting for the moment about her hidden charges.

But Brett wouldn't let her forget completely. "How's your worker?"

"Huh?"

"The one you took to the doctor today. The sick one."

"Oh, yes, she's fine. Er, I mean, she'll be okay soon."

"Is she sick enough to go back home?"

"Home?" Annie felt like laughing. Oh, how she *wished*! "She, uh, she expects to be back to work in a few days." Annie figured that explanation was probably near the truth.

"Good. Theresa's a darn good doctor." He reached for the door and held it open for her.

Annie slipped past him, catching a whiff of his masculine scent in the process. Being with Brett was a pleasant, no . . . a sensuous experience. With his exciting and dangerous past, chasing criminals and getting shot, he was even more intriguing to her.

Yet, the man she'd come to know in the past couple of days had the appealing attributes of being strong and steady. Plus, in his neat, stylish clothes, he was magnificent. Annie couldn't help but like him. Flipping the kitchen light on, she reminded herself that Brett Meyer wouldn't be here long. So, she'd better cool her emotions.

The kitchen was just as she'd left it this morning, including cold, stale coffee in the pot. She hadn't done anything all day except take care of those women. It irked her to think that they and their problems had dominated her time. And yet she felt compelled to help. Trying to forget them, Annie grabbed the coffeepot. "I guess I'll start here."

Brett reached around her, covering her hands with his. "I can do this part. Coffee's my speciality. Lots of practice over the years."

Annie smiled over her shoulder, enjoying the closeness. "Okay, I'll make the salad." She moved reluctantly out of the circle of his arms. What was happening here was a silent seduction, and she had better be aware of her own weakness in the presence of this man. He was extremely attractive in many ways. And she was vulnerable.

Still feeling the tingling sensations from his touch, Annie started on the salad. Her fingers shook slightly as she tore the lettuce, which she blamed on the fact that she hadn't eaten all day. But to be honest, she had to admit that one look from Brett could start her heart pounding. And his touch livened every cell in her being.

She chopped fresh mushrooms and credited her reactions to those of a lonely, love-starved woman. Brett was, indeed, an intriguing, alluring man. And she had to ignore her immature response to his obvious assets.

Working quickly, Annie put a plateful of potatoes into the microwave for baking and opened a can of green peas.

"You must be very hungry," Brett commented dryly. The coffee started sputtering through the drip system, and he leaned his hips on the counter and watched her.

"Oh, I am, but this isn't all for me. I'm, uh, going to feed Diego and the workers tonight."

"Do you always cook for them?"

"Well, one's been sick, remember."

"Right." His dark eyes assessed her. "Anything else I can do?"

She handed him plates and flatware. "Set the table."

They worked together to put the food on the table. Annie loaded a tray with some of everything and set it out on the back porch, as she'd promised Diego. Finally she sat down opposite Brett, gazed at the spread and sighed. "This looks great. Thanks for bringing the chicken, Brett."

He watched in awe as Annie heaped food onto her plate. "My pleasure entirely. Now, if you can eat all that, I'll really be impressed."

"Just watch me," she said. "I told you I was starved." As they began to eat, she attempted casual conversation, but with an underlying motive. "So, how are your friends, Manny and Dr. Theresa?" Maybe he'd give her a clue about whether Dr. Theresa had reported Annie's illegals. Now was the time for her to find out, before this went any further.

"Busier than ever. They admitted to an increased influx of 'foreign travelers,' as they call them. And it's a big concern." Brett hesitated before adding with a wry smile, "No, Annie, they didn't turn anyone in to me."

Annie flushed. She knew how his friends must feel with Brett—torn between the legal position that he stood for and the moral dilemma they felt in their hearts. "The whole problem is a big concern for us all. I suppose life must be quite difficult for families south of the border."

"Hey, times are tough all over. We aren't responsible for their country's turmoil." He split his baked potato and dropped a pat of butter into the middle.

Annie thought that his comment epitomized the man. Tough as nails. No sympathy. No leniency. How could she get along with a man like that? "What about the individual people who are struggling?"

"I, personally, feel sorry for them. But we have laws in this country that I've sworn to uphold."

Annie looked at him curiously. "But the laws don't take into account individual circumstances." She certainly didn't want to have an argument with him over this. Basically she agreed with him. This was her first experience in harboring anyone—and her last, she hoped. Still, she felt defensive of her actions.

"The laws are for the majority," he said as if that settled everything in his mind. He failed to notice, or failed to acknowledge, her discomfort. "What impressed me most was what Manny and Theresa said was happening to Silverton."

"And what's that?" What sensitive subject would he touch on next?

"It's growing," he said with a boyish smile and a palms-up gesture with both hands. "It's developing. New jobs are coming into town. Things are happening around here."

"You seem surprised." She was relieved with the new turn of the conversation. This was a subject dear to her heart.

"I'm amazed. I figured this old town would fold, like so many of the others, when the smelter closed. At one time, Manny and Theresa had even talked about moving to Colorado. I thought my dad was a figurehead sheriff. But he's actually doing something vital every day. He has a large, busy core of officers who are dealing with some serious problems."

"I don't know much about crime in this county," she admitted. "But I do know that we seldom see J.M. out here anymore. And everybody thinks he's doing a great job."

"He persuaded me to come home by saying he needed me." Brett took a few bites of his salad. "I figured he meant on the ranch, especially when I saw what a mess it was."

"He hasn't done one thing out there since your mother died, Brett. He seems to have lost any interest in it."

"The old place looks pretty bad. And I think that, deep down, my dad would like to see it become a working ranch again. But that's not the real reason he wanted me here."

Annie smiled sweetly. "Are you going to tell me he's just a softhearted father who wants his only son to get well and not to risk his life again?"

"Softhearted? That's a laugh!" Brett scratched his chin with his thumb and grinned sheepishly. "Naw, he has other ideas for me."

"Oh?" She began wiping her fingers on the napkin in her lap. When he didn't continue right away, she looked up at him, eyebrows raised, questioning.

"He wants to hire me as a special investigator, sort of a consultant on certain difficult crimes that the department has from time to time."

Annie dropped the napkin into her lap. "Like the increased numbers of illegal aliens?"

He shrugged. "That's probably one of the first things he wants me to investigate."

"Are you . . . going to do it?"

"Yes, I think I will. It means I'll be around for a while."

"Oh, good." Annie smiled weakly, her expression belying her words. Her emotions were split, too.

From the beginning, she'd wanted Brett to find their small-town atmosphere appealing enough to stick around for a while. Now that he was staying, he'd probably end up investigating her!

4

BRETT OBSERVED her reaction to his announcement.

Annie was giving him a series of mixed signals, and he couldn't understand why. Her eyes widened and flickers of light appeared in their sea-green depths, indicating some interest or curiosity. Contrarily, her lips, pink and luscious and oh-so-inviting, quivered ever so slightly, showing some hesitation at his announcement.

He decided to test her. "Good? That sounds sufficiently noncommittal."

"I'm surprised, that's all."

Brett tried to discern the real message in her eyes, but right now could only verify their deep green beauty. He noticed that suddenly her breathing seemed uneven and sort of jerky. She fiddled with her fork, a sure sign of nervousness.

He caught himself. What the hell was he doing, evaluating her like this? What next? A notebook, describing her physical reactions? This was no interview of a suspect. This was Annie . . . *Annie*, the woman he couldn't seem to get out of his mind.

In spite of the obvious benefits of being able to detect and possibly interpret certain body language, Brett actually hated this skill he used in his job. He found it impossible not to transfer the knowledge to personal relationships. He wished that he could just let nature take its course.

Unfortunately, Brett couldn't do that anymore. He had seen too much, been too far. With Annie, for instance, he found it difficult to just sit back and enjoy her. He was too impatient for that.

Although Brett kept his responses light, he knew that the decision to stay in Silverton was a serious one. "I guess I hoped to see more enthusiasm from you, Annie. Something to match mine."

"You're eager to stay?" She angled her head to the side and wrinkled her nose. "That's a switch. I thought you couldn't wait to leave this . . . Podunkville."

"A change of heart, you might say." Brett wondered if his revelation was really so startling as she seemed to indicate.

Annie took a sip of her coffee and licked her lips slowly. "I suppose that means you don't find us so dull and boring anymore?"

He laughed aloud. So that was it? She was still stinging from his initial reaction to coming home. Perhaps he *had* been rude. "That was arrogant of me," he said with an apologetic shake of his head. "Sorry if I offended you. To be honest, I haven't had time to get bored yet, because I've been too busy. I don't know how Dad figured being here would give me a chance to recuperate."

"It's refreshing to have a different atmosphere," she offered. "Sometimes a change works to heal the body as well as the spirit."

"Are you saying my spirit needs doctoring?"

"Not necessarily, Brett. But you *have* been through a lot. You probably just need a rest."

His dark eyes became even darker. "I need time to sort through why my partner died and I didn't."

Annie reached out and spontaneously squeezed his hand. "Don't waste your time searching for answers where there are none, Brett."

"What are you, an expert on such matters?"

"I've done my share of searching."

"Ah, you're right." He slapped his thigh and shook his head. "There are no easy answers to the hard questions of life. The hospital counselor said the same thing. All I can say about this place is that it's much safer here. I guess that's what my dad had in mind for me."

"And what did you have in mind, Brett?"

He pursed his lips. "I envisioned hours of nonactivity on a lounge chair in the sun, catching up on a few dozen paperback spy thrillers, maybe taking a little side trip or two."

Her eyes twinkled teasingly. "Like to San Francisco?"

"Yeah, with my next-door neighbor," he drawled, leaning back in his chair and stroking his chin. That loaded proposition probably still bugged her, too. "I realize now that's an impossibility. There's too much work to do around here. For you. And—" he paused to finish his coffee in a single gulp "—for me. A few days ago I couldn't see that. But a few days ago, I couldn't see a lot of things."

"Like the hard labor that has to be done on an apple farm or—" she paused to check his reaction "—or what needs to be done on a run-down cattle ranch to bring it up to par?" She rose and began clearing their plates. "If that's even remotely what you plan to do."

After a moment he followed her to the sink, carrying both their coffee cups. "Would you believe that I'm considering it? Remotely, that is."

Annie bent to open the dishwasher and began stacking plates inside. She knew the possibility of him hanging around for long, much less fixing up the old Rocking M Ranch was slim. "Don't make any rash statements for my benefit, Brett." She turned around, not realizing he was standing so close. "You haven't even been back a week yet. Maybe you've forgotten what this type of work is like." She took the cups from him and placed them in the dishwasher. "How hard it is."

"All work is hard, if it's worth anything."

She stood facing him, less than a reach away. "Sounds like a cliché you found in a self-help book."

"Came from my dad, actually. He had a few good platitudes." Brett hesitated, then went on. "I'll admit, though, that I had forgotten some of the country pleasures, too."

She chuckled. "Now that definitely *is* an overused cliché. You're going to say that I'm the best pleasure around here, right?"

He snapped his fingers. "Got me."

"Hey, I may look like a country bumpkin, but I've been around a little," she boasted.

"I'm sure you have," he said.

She countered, but he wasn't listening. He was watching her—fascinated.

She faced him with such a lovely innocence that all he could do was think what a delight it would be to kiss her. As those cat eyes flashed at him, he experienced a tight quickening in his loins. She continued to rail at him undaunted, even as desire spiraled through him, and he became preoccupied with her mouth. He imagined the gratification of applying his lips to the burgundy curve of hers.

Annie propped her fists on her hips. He admired the firm shape of her breasts as they rose and fell beneath her sweater. My, oh, my, she certainly was distracting.

"And if you think you're going to breeze in here for a few weeks and pretend to enjoy our peaceful little lifestyle.... And if you think you're going to sweep me off my feet, you're—Dammit, Brett! You aren't hearing a word I'm saying!" She caught her lower lip between her front teeth, thus preventing those luscious lips from being kissed.

"Oh, yes, I have," he lied. "No sweeping, I promise."

"Brett . . ." She sighed and shook her head at him. "All right, are there any more dishes?"

"That's it," he said without bothering to glance back at the table. He simply couldn't take his eyes off her. "You know, Annie, for a quiet country girl, you can be quite a spitfire." He took her hands loosely in his.

"Nobody claimed I was quiet." She tried to pull away, but he held her firmly.

"I guess that was my own fantasy of the girl next door." He placed her hands on his waist. "But you are a definite spark of energy around here."

"I would think you'd know that from growing up next door to me." She tried to fight the feelings that flooded her when they touched. His hands were wonderfully warm and strong as they clasped hers, and his aura seemed to embrace her.

"You were only there during summers. Anyway, I was blind to a lot of things when I was a kid. But now that I'm a man, I have a different perspective on many things. On life. On people. Even—especially—on you, Annie."

"Me?" She felt jittery inside, and a nervous twitch seemed to have invaded her breathing apparatus.

"On you and me, Annie. But I need to know—" He hesitated, realizing that he was sounding presumptuous. When it came to women, though, he had never been very sophisticated. "Uh, do you have a man in your life right now, Annie?"

"If I said yes, would you back off?"

He scanned her face for a moment. "No way. I'd just know what kind of fight I had on my hands." His loose-gripped caress slid up her arms. It was with great effort that he restrained himself from sweeping her against his aching body. "Is your answer yes?"

"No, not—"

Before she could finish, he cupped her chin in one hand and lifted it slightly. "Good. Because I'm definitely interested in the lovely apple farmer next door."

"Is that why you're staying, Brett? Because of me?"

With his other hand he circled her neck beneath the weight of her hair. "At this point, I can truthfully say that there are several reasons. One is to help J.M. I'm soft-hearted enough to believe that he needs me. Another is to catch the bad guys. I'm confident enough to believe I can make a difference. And the other reason—" he moved closer "—is to kiss the beautiful girl next door."

He bent to caress her lips softly, sensuously, with his.

As Annie stood there, eyes closed, lips slightly open, she felt like a dry fountain receiving life-giving mois-

ture. It had been a long drought, and she welcomed his
male vitality and strength.

Brett felt himself drawn into her innocence, almost as
if a spell were winding around them. Her lips were fan-
tastically soft and warm. And he felt the heat radiating
deep in his loins.

He lifted his head and smiled, enjoying watching her
responses to his preliminary advances. "And I'm arrogant enough to believe my lovely neighbor's enjoying it
as much as I am."

Annie's eyes flew open and she became instantly alert.
Her hands had been resting naturally on his chest and she
pushed on the muscular wall, trying to put some distance between them. "That may be so, but sometimes
physical enjoyment is short-lived."

He backed off and let her move away from him.
"What's wrong, Annie? You know you enjoyed it."

She turned around, her eyes staring with catlike intensity. "I don't trust you, Brett."

"Don't trust me?" He shrugged, palms out. "Hell, I'm
your neighbor, Annie. Your friend, I hope. I'm not going
to get out of line with you. I'll stop any time you say."

"I know." She switched her tactic. "I don't mean it like
that, Brett."

"Then, what?"

"You're the transitory type. One day, out of the blue,
you come back here, not really liking it, but promising
to hang around a while. You grab a quick kiss and maybe
more. Then, someday you'll get tired of us, say we're
boring and announce you're leaving. I don't want that in
a relationship."

He wanted her, but not at the risk of lying. He couldn't do that to Annie. "I can't promise anything long-term right now. I'm just trying to put the pieces together after nearly losing my life. Maybe Silverton is in my future. Maybe not."

"I understand. And I don't think anyone should pressure you. Or rush you into a decision. That goes for your father or me. But I want you to know where I stand, Brett." She folded her arms, feeling a certain security in the motion.

He gazed at her questioningly. "You've found your niche here in Silverton, New Mexico?"

To Annie, his query seemed to have a deeper significance, so she gave him more than a superficial answer. "I'm creating the kind of life I want here on the farm and in Silverton. I like what I'm doing. I've put a lot of work into this town. I fit in. And I like—this sounds silly—but I like *me*."

"So do I, Annie." He studied her for a moment. "I can't promise much at this point. But one thing I know. I could never use you." Hesitantly he lowered his head for one more sweet, sensitive kiss. Their lips matched and meshed, warmly transmitting unwarranted feelings and emotions.

Reluctantly Brett withdrew from her. He felt a tightness in his entire body. She was a powerful force, pulling on him like a magnet, and he wanted to stay close to her. He yearned for more than she was willing to give at this point, and he couldn't trust himself not to take it. Stiffly he moved to the door and grabbed his coat from the rack.

Annie watched him with sultry eyes. "Where are you going?"

"If I stay any longer, we both may regret it." He gazed at her solemnly. "And I don't want any regrets between us, Annie. None. I'll be back...."

"Tomorrow?" It was a spontaneous question.

"Well, I had planned to tackle the weeds before they take over my ranch. If you'd like, I'll be glad to drive the tractor over here and work on your weeds, too. Or whatever you need."

"I . . . sure." She nodded jerkily. "That sounds great."

He reached for the door.

"Brett?"

"Yeah?"

"Thanks for bringing supper. And for coming over. I needed company tonight. And I enjoyed yours very much."

"It seemed the neighborly thing to do." He smiled rakishly. "And the only way to spend a little more time with you, Annie. Whether you believe it or not, that's all I wanted tonight."

"And next week? What will you expect then, Brett?"

"Why don't we wait and see?" He grinned. "Wait and see what *you* want."

Annie opened her mouth to speak, then decided against whatever was on her mind. "Okay, it's a deal. See you tomorrow?"

"I'll try to make it before noon." With a quick nod, he was gone.

Annie watched his car lights disappear, thinking it curious that he aggravated her and excited her at the same time. Maybe the one she didn't trust here was herself, not Brett. She could admit privately that she was wildly attracted to the man. Maybe she was just attracted to men on the move, men who were great risks to her heart.

She hoped not, but she had to look at her record. There was Matt, who took a job in Boston. Their breakup was mutual, but it left her lonely for a long time. However, that heartbreak was mild compared to the one with Dan. They had been together for three years. One day he announced he was moving to Colorado. Annie was not invited.

And now, what about Brett? She hugged her arms, remembering the multitude of feelings she experienced when his lips met hers. Yes, the problem was definitely with her. She found him far too attractive. Far too alluring. Far too much of a man to resist.

BRETT DROVE the car slowly. He couldn't forget the way she looked when he touched her, the way her skin felt next to his, the warmth of her receptive lips. And he wanted more. Much more. He wondered if he had the guts to do whatever was necessary to have her. It might even mean lying to her.

Before he had an answer, he pulled into the driveway and found J.M. waiting for him. Sexy thoughts of Annie had to be shoved aside.

The two men greeted each other warmly with a combination handshake and half hug. "In the neighborhood, J.M.?" Brett asked, calling his father by his first name as he had since he was a kid.

"Sort of." J.M. grinned. "You visiting the neighbors?"

"I'm just a neighborly kind of guy," Brett said with a grin, refusing to answer directly. He ambled to the refrigerator. "Want a beer?"

"Have you got a soda? It wouldn't do for the sheriff to be caught with beer on his breath."

"Never thought I'd see you refuse a beer." Brett grabbed a cola for J.M. and a beer for himself. "Times have changed."

"Yep." J.M. popped the top of the canned drink and lifted it toward Brett in a mock toast. "This is what responsibility does for you."

"You make a good lawman," Brett said, returning the gesture. "Maybe it's what you should have done all along."

"You mean instead of struggling and failing at ranching all those years?" J.M. shrugged. "Maybe you're right, son. Hindsight is always best. I did it for—" He halted abruptly.

Brett picked up the trail of words. "I know. You did it for Mama."

J.M. nodded silently. After a moment, he asked, "How's Annie doing?"

"Pretty good. She didn't lose many blossoms in the freeze." Brett ambled into the front bedroom and motioned for his dad to follow him. "I don't think it'll hurt her crop much this year."

J.M. halted in the middle of the familiar room. It had been Brett's. Even after all these years, it still looked like a boy's room. "You could use the back bedroom, you know."

"Yours and Mama's room?" Brett asked sharply as he sat on the edge of the single bed and removed his boots.

"It's bigger." J.M. shrugged. "And the bed's bigger."

"No, thanks." Brett pulled off his socks. "My old room's fine."

"Lots of memories here." J.M. leaned on the door frame, his gaze circling the walls and ceiling. "This whole place reminds me—" His voice halted.

"Of Mama?" Brett sighed heavily. "Me, too."

"Do you...uh, mind staying here? Or would you prefer a place in town? I'm sure I can find you something...."

"No, Dad. This is fine." Brett peeled off his sweater and began to unbutton his shirt. He let it hang open casually in the front. "This is home."

"And I'm glad to have you back here, son."

"I'm going to fix this place up, J.M. You'll be surprised next time you come."

"You don't have to do anything out here, Brett."

"I know. But if I'm going to live in it, I want it in better shape than this." He laughed and gestured at the dirty walls and torn curtains. "I'm not a complete slob."

J.M.'s gaze went to his son's chest, visible beneath the open shirt. The long thin surgeon's scar was blurred at one end by the spot that marked the gunshot wound. J.M. took a sharp breath and turned away from the painful sight.

Brett followed him into the living room. "What's wrong?" He ran his hand lightly over the scars. "Hell, don't let a little flesh wound bother you. It's all healed now."

"I've seen a lot in my life," J.M. said, turning back with a sheepish grin. "Especially in the past three years as sheriff. But it's different when you see your own flesh 'n' blood torn up like that."

"Hey, it's not so bad now. I'm okay."

"You need to take it easy, Brett. You haven't stopped to rest since you got here."

"Now you *sound* like Mama." He paused to take a swig of beer. "Besides, there's lots to do here and at Annie's farm. I like to stay busy. Keeps me from thinking too much. Is this why you came all the way out here to-night? To tell me to take it easy?"

J.M. nodded and chuckled. "Take everything slowly, Brett. That includes Annie."

"Are you giving me advice on how to handle females?"

"Hell, no! I just figure if you've got any common sense in your head, you'll see what a great gal she is. And she's damn pretty, too."

"Thanks for pointing that out." Brett spread his legs and leaned his elbows on his knees.

J.M. ambled around the room. "The real reason I came out is to tell you that we don't need you to start on your projects with the department right away. Take your time, as much as you need."

"Thanks. I can't help wondering if you need me at all."

J.M. gave his son a quick response. "Oh, hell, yes, we need you. Or someone with your expertise. How often does an ex-FBI agent make himself available to a small county sheriff's department? We want to take advantage of you while you're here, Brett. It's just that we need a little time for the funds to come through for your salary. I figured you could use a little time, too."

"Sure. That'll give me a chance to do some things around here. And to help Annie a little."

"Yeah. Do that. Help Annie. She needs a man. Er, that is, she needs a man's strength. That girl's been doing the job of two or three since she took over the farm from old Martin."

Brett smiled at his dad's reference to Annie's needs. He couldn't agree more. With a wide yawn, he leaned back in the old stuffed chair. "Want to spend the night here with me, Dad?"

"No! No, thanks. I've gotta get back to town. Just stopped by to chat." J.M. set his empty can on a table.

"What's wrong? Too many ghosts around here for you?"

"I guess so. Especially at night." He adjusted his large white cowboy hat on his graying crown. "You take care, now. And I'll see you in a couple of weeks. I don't expect you to report for work before that. In fact, I'll let you know."

"Okay," Brett agreed, standing to hug his father.

"Get some rest, son."

"Yessir."

Brett watched J.M.'s truck lights disappear in the darkness, then he cut the house lights, stripped off his clothes and heaved himself tiredly into bed. So the real truth was coming out. This house held too many memories of the past and J.M.'s beloved Rosa for him to spend much time here.

As he relaxed, Brett ran his hand automatically over his chest and down to stroke the scar. He smiled in the darkness, remembering J.M.'s reaction to the sight of it. He was a tough man, reluctant to show his feelings. But tonight Brett had seen signs of the affection J.M. felt for his son and for his departed wife. Brett remembered his teen years, spent in this very room, when he wondered if his old man loved anyone.

Those were hard years for everyone. Brett was growing up and struggling for his place in the scheme of things. J.M. was struggling financially to support his family on the ranch. Finally he had taken a job at the copper smelting plant. When it closed a few years ago, J.M. had sought the county sheriff's position.

Now Brett understood that J.M. did love him and his mother very much. He just had trouble showing it. Sometimes, being macho got in the way.

Brett didn't linger long on the past. As he drifted off to sleep, his subconscious wandered to a certain spunky neighbor with strawberry-blond hair and sea-green eyes and the sweetest kiss this side of heaven. And he wanted her again. More than ever.

FOR THE NEXT WEEK, Brett divided his work between Annie's farm and his ranch, giving her the lion's share of his energy. She didn't quite understand why, but she wasn't about to question his motives. She only knew that she needed extra hands and that Brett worked diligently, often from early morning until sunset. At dusk, he left. There were no more boxed suppers and no pressures for her to respond to his presence.

By keeping him busy in the fields, it was easier for Annie to hide her unwanted guests. It also gave her the opportunity to prepare the kinds of foods Dr. Theresa had recommended for Isabel.

Annie developed a routine of bringing Brett's lunch. Often she ate with him. It was a way of keeping him away from the house and possibly discovering her illegal guests. But also, she realized, it was a time when they could be alone, and she enjoyed that very much.

In a way, she was a little disappointed by his curtailed pursuit. Being pursued by the likes of Brett Meyer might have been fun. On the other hand she was angry at herself for even feeling that way. She knew that he was only responding to her tough-sounding speech about him breezing into her life, thinking he could land in her bed. Right now, that didn't sound too bad. And yet, she knew that she didn't want another fleeting love affair.

Annie pulled the Jeep to a stop and watched Brett as he drove the tractor and disk expertly between the Red Delicious rows. He had removed his shirt in the midday heat and tied it around his waist, leaving his bare chest and muscular back exposed for her admiration. When he completed the row and headed back toward her, she beeped the horn and waved to him.

Brett lifted his arm and indicated that he would join her when he got to the end of the row. Annie grabbed the small cooler containing their lunch and headed for the shade of one of the older trees.

She waited and watched as Brett finished the row, then stopped the tractor. With surprising agility he hopped to the ground, his shirt flapping about his lean hips. He walked around the tractor to get a drink from the large water cooler riding on the other side of the cab.

She had a full view of him, and her gaze dropped to his rib cage in search of the scar. He hefted the cooler and turned it up, letting the water spill into his mouth and run down his neck and chest. Captivated by the erotic sight, Annie could almost see the steam rising from his heated body.

By the time he reached her, Brett had donned his shirt and partially buttoned it. He was the most sexy and ruggedly handsome man she had seen in a long time, and she made no effort to hide her admiration.

"What's wrong?" he challenged when he was close enough to notice. "My fly unzipped?"

She flushed. That wasn't supposed to embarrass her. But it did. "Can't I admire a good-looking man?"

"Now *that's* a cliché if I ever heard one!" It was his turn to be embarrassed. She could swear his face darkened as he started digging into the lunch cooler for food. "Damn good thing I like apples," he drawled with a teasing glance her way. He pulled out several apple slices stuck together with peanut butter and began to chomp them hungrily. "Who taught you to cook, anyway?"

"That's the great thing about apples," she countered. "You don't have to cook them in order to enjoy them."

"Then you're in luck. Real men eat them raw." He handed her an apple quarter.

"Hey, nobody's complained about my cooking before." She licked daintily at the peanut butter on the apple.

"That's because nobody's eaten anything you fixed."

"What about that *pozole* the night of the big freeze?"

He nodded. "Excuse me. You're absolutely right. That *pozole* was fantastic. You are a good cook."

"When I have somebody to appreciate my efforts, I'm fair."

"Oh, you're never just fair, Annie. You're great! And I appreciate every effort you make," he pledged. "Like this lunch, for instance." He opened another plastic sandwich bag and pulled out a thick slice of her famous apple bread. Taking a bite, he mumbled, "Mmm, this is more like it. Now, this is great stuff. What's in it?"

"Apples." She laughed.

He bent toward her and examined her closely with devilishly dark eyes. "Did you make it?"

"Of course! Who do you think? Diego?"

"Well, I didn't know."

"It's an old family recipe," she added with a sniff. "I don't hand it out to just anybody. I usually *sell* it. But for a select few, I make exceptions."

"A select few, huh?" He gestured toward his midsection. "And I'm one of those?"

"Sure are." She smiled sweetly. "It's nice to have you here, working for me. That's why I fix you lunch. I'd like to keep you around. You're good for my farm, Brett. I almost didn't make it last year, but this year, I can see red and golden profits growing on the trees."

"I almost didn't make it last year, either," he said with a wink. "Maybe we'd both have been better off if I'd hired on to help at the farm a year or so ago." He picked a spot and sat on the ground beside her.

"Maybe so..." The bantering between them had cooled. By spending so much time together, they were getting to know each other, learning how and when to tease, sharing a few laughs.

Annie placed her hand on his arm. "You're the best thing I've seen around here in a long, long time, Brett. A hero is rare in these parts."

"You know how I feel about this hero stuff."

"No, how?"

Suddenly he turned serious. "Is my partner any less a hero because he died in the same battle that gave me this nebulous status?"

"Of course not." She was a little startled at his abrupt change. But she remembered her own crazy emotions, spiking from high to low and level again during the time when she was grieving heavily for her beloved aunt and uncle. "Are you feeling guilty, Brett?"

"Maybe." He turned away from her. The day had been too perfect. He enjoyed being with Annie too much. He liked working for her, seeing the results of his labor, seeing her face light up with pleasure.

Tilling the soil today, turning over weeds, getting back to the earth had made him feel good. Too good. The midday sun felt warm and seductive on his body. And relaxing. They were sensuous pleasures his partner would never enjoy again.

Being with Annie was his life support. She made him glad to be alive. He even had a job in town, a reason for being. Everything was moving along nicely. That was the trouble. It was too nice and tidy. Maybe that was what pushed his emotions to the surface today with her.

"Guilty?" he repeated with a growl. "Guilty for living? Hell, yes! Maybe now, today, more than a little guilty."

"Why is today so bad, Brett? Memories?"

"Oh, Annie, today isn't bad. It's good. Too good. These days...this time...with you has been great. I know it sounds crazy, but the better things are going, the worse it gets in here." He placed a fist in the center of his chest. "I thought it would fade in time. But it hasn't. I thought time would heal this damned aching I feel. But nothing's changed."

Annie empathized with him, hurt for him.

She touched his cheek, stroking gently until he turned toward her. Gazing into his sad, dark eyes, she murmured, "I wish I could kiss away the pain." She leaned forward and kissed both of his cheeks. "But I know I can't do that." She kissed his lips softly.

"Annie..."

"I can only kiss you, Brett, and tell you that I'm sorry about your partner and all the pain you've been through. And I'm sorry about your job with the FBI, because obviously you loved it. But, I'll admit, I'm very glad you're here with me." Her lips passed over his, lightly stroking, sipping, kissing.

It was the first time she had made such an aggressive move toward him. But that didn't matter now. Only feelings did. And her openhearted response to his outpouring. Her lips sought his, pressing solidly, teasing them apart with the tip of her tongue. With a genuineness she couldn't express in words, her passionate actions told him what he needed to hear, needed to feel. She cared.

When Annie finally lifted her head to take a deep breath, they were lying on the ground. Her breasts were crushed against his chest. His arms had encircled her back. Both seemed to be a little startled to find themselves sprawled together under the apple blossoms.

"Brett, I didn't mean to—" She scrambled to a sitting position. "I don't know what came over me."

"I think that's my line." He hopped to his feet and pulled her against him. "I'd better get back to work. Before the boss catches me lying down on the job."

She grinned. "Yeah. Me, too."

Brett kissed her nose, then headed for the tractor, feeling better than he'd believed possible a few minutes ago.

Yes, Annie had something special. And it seemed to be just what he needed.

5

"CARMEN'S SICK?"

Diego stood in the dark doorway, hat in hand, nodding silently.

"Great. Just great." Annie groaned and turned back into the kitchen. "Come on in and have some coffee. Tell me about it. Does she need to see the doctor, too?"

"I don't think that is necessary. She just cannot come with us now."

Annie was more than a little agitated by Diego's announcement. This morning they were supposed to be taking Isabel to Dr. Theresa for more blood tests. "What's wrong with her?"

Head down, Diego walked over to the coffeepot and poured himself a cup. "She just says she is not feeling well today. But please, could you take Isabel for her tests?"

"Sure. Yes. Of course." Annie drank the last of her coffee and set the cup into the sink. Pink fingers of daylight were beginning to stretch across the gray morning sky. "I can't believe they both came into this country sick."

"Things were difficult in their troubled country," Diego said soberly. "They came here looking for a better life."

"Yeah, I guess." Annie gazed at Diego for a moment. Of course, he must have talked with them in their native language about their journey and the reasons for leaving their homeland. She hoped they had a plan for continuing their journey past Silverton, New Mexico. "Well, we'll do our best with Isabel and hope Carmen feels well enough to travel soon. I want them gone before—" she paused and sighed "—before someone like Brett Meyer catches them here."

"*Sí, señorita.*"

"Speaking of Brett, he's supposed to come back and work today. Did he finish with the tractor and disk?"

"Oh, yes. Turned over every spare inch of soil. And he did a pretty good job, too."

"You seem surprised, Diego."

A smile creased his dark face. "I keep thinking of him as that pesky kid next door who used to steal apples from your uncle and throw them at his dad's cattle. No wonder poor J.M. never made it on that ranch. His cattle were always spooked. They were probably tough as old leather."

"Maybe that's why Brett's working so hard for us now. He wants to make up for his little sins of the past."

"I think he has more in mind these days than making up for a few stolen apples." The old man grinned knowingly at her.

"For someone so busy, you certainly are observant of things that are none of your business, Diego." She picked up the towel and took a few nervous swipes at the counter around the sink. "Whatever Brett's reasons are, we'll accept his help as long as he's available. Which probably won't be long." In spite of what Brett had said, she still couldn't believe he was here to stay.

"I am not complaining. We can use a good, strong back around here."

"Frankly, I wasn't sure if Brett would be much help, considering his injury." She wouldn't soon forget the bold image of Brett sitting on the tractor the other day. The way his bare shoulders and muscular chest gleamed with sweat in the midday sun.... "But it doesn't seem to affect his work."

"He is strong," Diego concluded.

Annie nodded curtly, not really wanting to pursue the topic of Brett Meyer. She hadn't forgotten the effects of his touch and that kiss she had willingly given him—the way it had turned so magical.... "Uh, Diego, did you finish weeding all the orchards?"

"Yes. Everything is under control. We're ready to start thinning the blossoms."

"What about the leaky irrigation pipe?"

"That is not under control," he admitted with a rueful shake of his head. "I think it is leaking in several places now. Maybe some animal exposed the pipe. And the winter weather did the rest."

"Well, I don't want to start thinning blossoms until we fix the pipes. We have to get our watering system in good working order or nothing will grow." She sighed heavily. "I'm afraid that whole stretch of pipe west of the Jonathan orchard will have to be replaced. I considered letting Foster Mayhill work on it, since he installed the system, but of course, the warranty is up, and I'd have to pay him plumber's wages. I wonder if you and I could fix it, with Brett's help."

"Of course. No problem. First we have to dig up the pipe."

She smiled grimly. "Okay, if you think we can do it, go ahead and start digging this morning. I'll get the pipe from the hardware store while I'm waiting for Isabel to have her tests. Dr. Theresa said the glucose tolerance test takes about three hours, so we'll be gone most of the morning."

"As soon as Brett gets here, we'll dig up the old pipe."

"Good deal." She grabbed her jacket from the rack by the door and started out, sliding her arms into the sleeves as she went. "Tell Isabel we'd better be going, Diego."

In a few minutes, he was helping Isabel into the truck, chatting with her in Spanish. Annie started the motor and looked at the older woman. *"Buenas días, Isabel. ¿Cómo estas?"*

"Bien, gracias."

"Bien," Annie responded, wishing she could say more. The only other Spanish phrases that readily came to mind were *¿Donde esta el baño?*, "Where is the bathroom?" and *Dos cervezas, por favor*, "Two beers, please." Neither of those would do now, so Annie smiled politely and shifted into gear. Isabel looked much healthier than she had a week ago. She was moving under her own power, no longer running a fever, and her leg was starting to heal. Annie figured the woman had to feel better.

The two bounced along in silence as they traveled the dirt road. Annie glanced at Isabel occasionally with a cheerful smile. It occurred to her that Isabel might be frightened and probably had no idea what was happening today. So she tried to think of a few more Spanish words that might reassure her. "Doctor Theresa *es bien*, uh, *médico*," she began hesitantly, then mumbled aloud,

"I'm assuming you know you're going back to the doctor."

"*Sí,*" Isabel offered tentatively.

"*Sí?* Are you understanding me?" Annie was delighted with a response from the silent woman. "How can I let you know that the doctor will make you feel better?" she muttered. "Uh, *mejor pierna.*" She laughed at herself. "'Better leg' sounds ridiculous. You can't possibly understand what I mean by that. Brother Harry, this is hard. I wish Carmen were here to interpret for me."

"She would come, if not so early. She sick every morning like this."

Annie slowed the truck and gazed at her passenger in amazement. "You speak English?"

"*Poco.* A little."

"Why didn't you tell me?"

"You not ask." Isabel smiled impishly. "Anyway, you were giving me *alegria*, much funny."

"Much funny? I bet." Annie shook her head and laughed. "All along you've understood. Well, at least you know Dr. Theresa wants to help you feel better. And make your leg well."

"Yes, better leg." Isabel covered her mouth and giggled.

Annie stared at the road for a minute before she was fully struck by all that Isabel had said. And what she meant. "Did you say that Carmen had...oh, Lord..." Annie held her breath. "Morning sickness?"

Isabel smiled sweetly. "It is the baby."

"Baby? Oh, brother! This is great! Just great! You have diabetes and Carmen's pregnant!" She sighed heavily. Annie's notion that her problems with these women were almost solved flew out the window. The problems were just beginning! "Now, what in heaven's name am I going to do with you?"

"We will be leaving soon."

"You're darn straight, you will." Annie gripped the steering wheel and clamped her teeth together. In only a few short minutes she had learned more about these two women than she ever wanted to know. And, although her first thought was to see them on their way, she wondered where they'd be going in their conditions. And who would help them . . . if anyone?

Annie left Isabel at the clinic and ran her errands. It was nearly noon when they returned to the farm. She'd bought hamburgers for everyone, including Diego and Brett, but when she saw that the men had not arrived for lunch yet, she went with Isabel to Diego's quarters to see how Carmen was feeling.

Isabel hugged the girl, then exchanged a few comments with her in Spanish. Annie stood silently, not fully understanding the words that tripped off their tongues. Finally Carmen turned to Annie. "Thank you for taking such good care of her."

"I discovered that Isabel speaks English." Annie gave Carmen a curious glance. "I just assumed she didn't."

"She is shy. But she understands."

"So I see. And how are you feeling, Carmen?"

Carmen sat on the edge of the bed, looking weak and pale. "I am all right."

"Have you eaten today? I brought some lunch. Would you like a hamburger?"

"What is it?"

Annie smiled and thrust the sandwich toward the slender girl. "Try it. American food."

With shaky hands, Carmen reached out. *"Gracias."*

Annie figured the girl hadn't eaten all morning. "It isn't good for your baby if you go so long without eating like this, Carmen. Go ahead and eat." She motioned at herself. "Isabel and I already ate our hamburgers. She was very hungry, since the doctor had instructed her not to eat all morning because of the tests."

Carmen took a tentative bite. In a few seconds, she smiled. "It is good, this hamburger."

"I thought you'd like it." Annie felt a certain satisfaction watching Carmen eat, and told herself she was suffering some sort of misplaced mothering syndrome. She even found herself giving practical advice. "You have to feed yourself well so your baby will grow strong. You both have to eat the right foods now. And you should let Dr. Theresa check on you, just to make sure everything is all right."

"How is Isabel?" Carmen asked.

"As Dr. Theresa suspected, Isabel has a disease called diabetes. She has to choose her foods from a list the doctor gave her. No more sugar. And she will have to take a pill every day for the rest of her life."

"And the pill will make her better?"

"It will keep her well." Annie sat on the bed near Carmen. "How will you do this? It's expensive and you're going to be traveling again soon."

Carmen lifted her head proudly. "When my Thomas comes for us, we will have the money for her medicine."

"Thomas?" Annie realized she was getting insight into a possible plan for the future. "He's coming for you?"

"Oh, yes. He does not even know about the baby." Carmen touched her stomach gently. "He will be so happy."

Privately Annie wondered how Thomas was going to take care of his sick mother and his pregnant wife. "When is he going to meet you? And where? Here?"

"At the ruins," Carmen said solemnly. "We were separated on the journey through Mexico. He always said to go to the mission."

"The mission ruins in the back of my property?" Annie's voice grew along with her alarm. "But how would he know about that?"

"The old mission is in stories, even songs. Everyone knows of it."

Annie was astounded. "And everyone uses them? Hiding, like you did?"

"Some. Not all."

Annie shivered. How many times had she been out there by herself? How many times had she *felt* a presence? And she'd foolishly thought it was her aunt's spirit. But why wouldn't Feliz bark at strangers?

"I can't believe my property has been used as a landmark for illegals."

"Please, do not tell anyone." Carmen put her hand on Annie's arm. "We will be leaving as soon as my Thomas comes for us."

Annie's gaze softened. "I won't tell anyone about you. But I can't have people trailing from Mexico through my property. It's . . . it's against the law. I could be fined. Or worse." She stood. "I hope your husband comes soon, Carmen. Do you know when the baby is due?"

"Not exactly. He is kicking a lot."

"Kicking? That means you're probably five months along or more. Oh, brother!" Annie heard the sound of the Jeep. Diego and Brett were returning for lunch. "We have company. It's Brett Meyer, my neighbor whose father is the sheriff," she said clearly. "Now, you two stay out of sight."

"*Sí señorita,*" they agreed in unison.

Annie dashed out of the shed, smoothing her clothes and trying to get a grip on herself as she went. Thoughts of seeing Brett made her excited and anxious at the same time. She was getting accustomed to seeing his handsome face on a daily basis and had actually missed him this morning when she had to take Isabel into town.

When she spotted him, though, she halted abruptly and stared in amazement. Was it actually Brett? The bare-chested man climbing out of the Jeep was absolutely filthy. Sweat had mingled with dirt on his body and jeans. There were dried mud freckles all over his bare flesh. His jeans were smeared with both wet and dry mud. His fashionable boots were no longer shiny; in fact, she couldn't tell if they were gray or brown.

And yet, as she gazed at him, Annie thought he was the most rugged, perhaps the most erotic-looking man she had ever seen.

He ambled toward her, his shirt tied to his hips and flapping in the breeze. "Hi. I hope you have a hose."

"Over by the house." Her mouth went dry.

"That must be where Diego went."

"You . . . you've ruined your boots."

"I hope not." He lifted each one to assess the damage. "I think they'll wash clean."

"Brett, uh . . ." Her voice trailed off as she forgot what she had intended to ask him. In that moment, irrigation pipes and refugees and apple blossoms and everything in her complicated world escaped her—everything except the sight of him. All Annie could think of was the way he looked, so noble and bold and copper colored. So naturally masculine.

Her gaze traveled from the muscled expanse of his shoulders to his smooth, hairless chest, past his rib cage to a long, awful scar. The red line curved halfway around his body. "Oh, Lord, Brett . . ."

"It looks much worse than it is, Annie," Brett said quietly when he saw her reaction.

Blood drained from her face, and she felt slightly weak-kneed. "I'm sure that's not true, Brett. You spent weeks in the hospital because of that." Her voice grew hoarse. "You almost lost your life because of it."

He brushed the scar lightly. "It's my badge of honor. It merited a call from the veep. And a pat on the fanny as I was royally ushered out."

"I can't say that I'm sorry. The FBI's loss is my, er, our gain."

"There's another of those overworked clichés."

"I mean it, Brett. I'm really glad you decided to come back home. I don't know what I'd have done this spring without all your help."

"Why, I'm sure you'd have managed, Annie."

"But not very well." She gestured at his filthy body. "Did you dig down to the old pipe?"

"We sure did. And did you bring a new one?"

"Yes. If you're ready, we can start on it after lunch. I bought fast-food hamburgers. Hope you don't mind."

"Did you say *we* can start?"

"Of course. It's my pipe, isn't it?"

"Well, yes. But this is a messy business."

"Hey, I've been messy before. I'll bet I get messier than you!" she challenged with a laugh.

"You're on! Now point me in the direction of the hose so I can get a layer or two of this stuff off before it sinks in."

She reached inside the truck and grabbed the bag of hamburgers, then walked with him toward the house. She pointed out the hose and headed for the porch, intending to change clothes while the men ate. Pausing on the step, she stole a glance at Brett splashing water over himself. Her insides twisted into a knot as she watched, fascinated, and envious of every drop that rolled down his gorgeous brown body.

When he finally joined her, she said, "I thought I'd never see that."

"Me washing with a hose?"

"Your boots. Dirty."

He looked puzzled. "Is that significant?"

"You bet it is," she said with a smile. How well she remembered his shiny boots and spiffy clothes. Maybe he was gradually adjusting to country life.

FOR THE NEXT FEW DAYS the three of them worked long and hard to replace the faulty pipe. Annie put on her jeans and rubber boots and got dirty alongside Diego and Brett. When the system was finally working properly, they rejoiced. But before they could rest, they had to move on to the next job, which was physically easier, but no less important.

"Large orchards use chemicals for thinning, but I prefer to do mine by hand," Annie explained.

Brett's gaze swept the orchard directly behind them. "Looks like a slow, tedious job to me."

"It's slow. But not tedious. Not to me, anyway. That's because I like to work with my hands." She spread them and shook her head sadly. "Which is why they look this way. I tried to wear work gloves for a while, but this is something that must be done very carefully by the feel. Like this."

He watched her hands move quickly over the clusters of blooms, eliminating all but one. "How do you know which one to leave?"

She moved to another cluster. "In the cluster of five or six, you trim to the center. Leave the largest, which is called the king bloom. Theoretically the trees produce best with one apple every forty leaves. Now you try it."

Brett's large hands covered the blooms, and he flicked them as she had done. Or so he thought. But when he was through, *no* blossoms remained. He cursed. "I must have gotten them all. What did I do wrong?"

"Here, like this," she explained patiently. She put her hand on his and directed his motions. Clumsily he flicked off two, three, four blossoms. "That's better. Now, try it."

He did. Again and again. Each time, he took too many. Or he left two and had to struggle to get a grip on one solitary blossom. It was terribly time-consuming. And frustrating for him. Annie could see this wasn't going to work.

Finally she said, "It's all right, Brett. Diego and I will do it."

"Do you mean I've failed blossom-thinning?" He feigned a hurt expression.

"Obviously it's not a job for everyone." She laughed and squeezed his hand. "It isn't a tragedy, you know. Your hands are just too big. Why don't you take a little break from apple farming, Brett? You probably need the rest."

"But what about you? You aren't stopping to rest, are you?"

"Not at this stage." She continued to thin the blossoms as she talked.

"Annie, this is too slow. At this rate, you'll be thinning blossoms all summer long."

"No, we won't. They won't last that long. They have to be done in the next few weeks. Then the apples start growing fast. It's an exciting time."

He frowned at her, but devilish lights danced in his dark eyes. "Watching apples grow is exciting?"

"Yep." She grinned good-naturedly. "You wait and see."

"Hey, I've been looking forward to a little excitement around this place."

"I'm sure it isn't your kind of excitement, Brett."

"And what kind is that?" He reached for the clump of blossoms on the next limb.

"Oh, bright lights, fast music, beautiful women." She heard him curse under his breath and looked up to see if he was reacting to her comment or having more trouble with the tiny, delicate apple blossoms. "Please don't, Brett. I'll get them."

"You can't get them all."

"Yes, I can. Diego will help. We did it last year without you."

"Now I'm hurt. You'd better use me while you can."

"There'll be other things for you to do. I promise. Please don't try any longer. I can't spare more apples. This is worse than the frost."

"Oh! You cut to the quick!"

"Sorry. But I have to save my apples." She sandwiched his hand between hers. His hand felt warm and strong, but not quite as smooth as a week ago. The palm contained a hard ridge where calluses were beginning to form, and she thought she detected a blister on one pad. The fingers were scratchy and rough to her skin. And yet, there was something secure about his hand, and she wanted to press it to her heart.

"It's difficult to find men who are good at this," she said. "That's probably one reason the big growers use chemicals to thin the blooms. It's time-consuming this way. I usually hire women because they have smaller hands and a more delicate touch."

"I guess that leaves me out."

"It's okay. You need a break. Now, go home and get some rest. We've been working you pretty hard lately."

He stuffed his hands into his back pockets and looked around. "You've got a helluva job ahead of you, Annie."

She shrugged. "I've done it before. Go on, now. Remember all those spy novels you wanted to read? Well, go read them." She released his hand and shooed him off with a little wave.

He started backing away. "Tell you what. I'll fix dinner tonight so you won't have to go home and cook. Just come over to my house when you're finished with work."

Annie knew she should refuse the offer. It was too appealing; *he* was too appealing. Spending an evening alone with him would be to run an emotional risk. Deep down, she feared he would be gone before the autumn harvest. And yet, as she looked into his dark eyes, she knew there was no way she could refuse him. Not right now. "Dinner sounds great, Brett."

"Come around seven. No take-out fried chicken this time, I promise."

"Can you cook?"

"I'll learn." He winked and was off.

Annie smiled after him, wishing time would fly so she could get to Brett's quicker. But as she turned back to her work, she knew that without help, she and Diego faced many hours of work. Last year she had hired several migrants for this job of thinning, but most of them weren't much better than Brett. This year she couldn't afford to hire anyone at all. She reached for another cluster.

Annie worked until nearly dark and then realized her guests needed a nutritious dinner. When she got in from the orchard, Isabel was preparing turkey enchiladas and Carmen was setting the table. It was the first time they had taken the initiative to go into her house and work.

"Diego said it would be all right if we started dinner," Carmen explained in an apologetic tone. "I hope you don't mind."

"It's fine as long as no one comes around. But you'd better check with me before you become so visible."

"*Sí*. That is wise."

"It looks great, but don't fix a plate for me, thanks," Annie said, grabbing a clean towel from the laundry room.

"Are you having company?" Isabel asked.

"No, I've been invited out for dinner. But you two go ahead and eat. Be sure to fix a plate for Diego."

"Are you going to see the sheriff's son?"

"Yes." Annie noted a strained look on both the women's faces. "Don't worry. I won't mention you."

Carmen smiled. "*Gracias*. We just want to help you because you've done so much for us. And we can do so little right now."

"Oh, that's all right. I never expected—" She halted and looked at the two women. "You want to help me?"

They both nodded eagerly.

"Are you serious? Have you ever thinned apple blossoms?"

They shook their heads simultaneously. And from the expressions on their faces, Annie knew they had no idea what she was talking about.

"It's simple. And it takes small, careful hands. I'll show you tomorrow. Maybe you *can* help me a little bit, after all."

"We would be happy to do anything for you." Isabel stepped forward. "As you can see, we are not sick anymore. And we are not helpless."

"Thanks. I appreciate it." Annie smiled gratefully. "Gotta go now. We'll start early tomorrow."

IT WAS NEARLY SEVEN-THIRTY before she arrived at the Rocking M. The savory fragrance of chili greeted her at the door. Even though Brett hadn't started making repairs to the old house, it was beginning to take on a homey atmosphere. Maybe it was just having someone here to use the place that made it seem so warm and livable again.

The meal Brett served was simple fare of chili and corn chips, topped with cheddar cheese and hot salsa. Annie even enjoyed the beer. "This was excellent," she said as they finished and began clearing the table. "And you said you couldn't cook."

"My culinary skills are limited. Coffee is at the top of the list, followed closely by chili. After that, the list is short."

"Having someone fix dinner for me after a long day's work was a real treat, Brett. You won't hear any complaints from me."

"I'm really sorry about the mess I made with the thinning."

"Don't worry about it. I found some help—" Annie halted abruptly. She must not be thinking straight tonight to have told him that.

"Oh? Who? Migrants?"

"Yes. Some, uh, migrant women came around needing jobs."

"The same one who was sick?"

She had hoped he had forgotten about that, but no such luck. "Uh, yes. She's much better now."

"Good. I'm glad you have help with the thinning."

"We should be finished in a few weeks."

"Now that I've lost my job at Annie's Apple Farm, I have another project." Brett changed the subject, much to Annie's relief.

"I thought you were going to rest. Relax and read." She felt very uneasy talking to Brett about the illegal women. And she disliked the lie she was perpetrating. She just could not worm her way out of the situation. Unfortunately, one lie seemed to lead to another, and she hated it.

"Too boring. I need to be busy."

"To keep you out of trouble?"

"You might say that." He fixed a pot of coffee. "I'm going to start cleaning and painting around here."

"Is that for J.M.'s benefit?"

"No. It's for mine. I want to make the place more livable since I'm going to be staying."

Annie glanced quickly at him, unable to hide the doubt in her expression.

"I swear, I'm staying long enough to enjoy it."

He was staying? And enjoying it yet? Was that conviction she saw in those dark eyes?

By the time the coffee was finishing brewing, they had washed the dishes. "Let's go into the living room," he suggested. "I'll show you what I'm doing in there."

"Okay." She helped him with the coffee cups.

He arranged a little plate of gourmet cookies and offered an apology. "They're from the store. I can't compete with your apple bread."

She tasted one. "They're pretty good."

He ate a cookie as he walked around the room. "I want to start in here. I did a little cleaning this afternoon, just to see what shape the place is in. The walls and fireplace need replastering. I thought your friend Holt could help me, or at least advise me on what to do and how to go about it."

"I'm sure he'd be glad to." Annie followed him. "He's especially interested in restoring old, quality buildings. I've always loved your beautiful beehive fireplace."

"And look at this." Brett knelt down and peeled back a corner of the carpet. "There's Mexican adobe tile under here. I'm going to rip up this old carpet and go back to the original tile flooring."

Annie bent to look over his shoulder and caught his masculine fragrance. The scent was as mesmerizing as the man. "Why, it's beautiful, Brett. Looks to be in good shape, too."

He straightened. "It should be. It's been protected by carpeting for as long as I can remember." He motioned across the long, narrow living room. "I can't decide what to do about the furniture. It's old and practically worn out, and I'd really like to get a different style. But this was my mom's choice, and I can't just toss it out."

She leaned forward with a smile. "Is that a sentimental statement I'm hearing?"

"I'm afraid so. See, even FBI agents have a soft heart when it comes to their mamas. We have feelings, too."

They were standing very close. Annie felt drawn to him and wrapped in his embrace even before he touched her. "I never doubted you had feelings, Brett." She had seen an honest display of his emotions the other day in the orchard when she had been moved to kiss him.

"I think you doubt my feelings for you, Annie." His hands touched her arms as he drew her closer. "I'm not sure I understand it, but I can't get you out of my mind. And all I can think of is kissing you again."

"I know what you mean."

His lips brushed hers softly. "Then you have these feelings, too? Feelings like I can't spend another night without you?"

"Uh-huh." She couldn't admit that she was fighting them every step of the way. As his mouth met hers and she opened her lips slightly to receive his kiss, Annie realized she was losing that battle. She wanted the kiss as much as he did. And she let him know it.

When his mouth molded sensuously to hers, Annie leaned into him, relishing the inherent strength of the man. His lips caressed hers, coaxing them open so that his tongue could edge her lips and dip inside. Her heart pounded a happy rhythm as swirls of delight radiated throughout her being. She wriggled into the welcome haven of his arms.

Responding to her willingness, Brett pulled her fully against him, sliding one hand to the curve of her back just above her buttocks. When he pressed, he could feel her against the heated ridge of his manhood. Just looking at her sometimes brought forth a strong masculine response, but holding her like this, feeling her against him, sent a surge of passion through him that traveled like lightning and felt like wildfire. Oh, how he wanted her! Tonight. As if to test her passion, his tongue plunged deeper.

Suddenly, like a double beacon, two beams of light flashed into the living room.

It took Brett a moment to pull himself back to reality. Headlights in the driveway. He lifted his head from her sweetness. "Annie . . . someone's here." He glanced quickly out the window and groaned. "It's J.M."

Immediately Annie pushed away. "I . . . I'd better be going."

"Not yet. We haven't finished . . . our coffee." His gaze caught hers with a special intensity. *Please don't go*, it seemed to say.

Just as J.M. knocked, she shook her head. "I must." Didn't he understand? If she stayed much longer, there'd be no turning back. Right now, she wasn't sure if she could handle such intimacy in her relationship with Brett. She needed more than time; she needed to be sure about him.

Brett greeted his father politely, but with the uncomfortable little silence that followed, Annie knew that J.M. could well guess what he had interrupted. Brett cleared his throat, and Annie touched her lips, hoping they didn't reveal signs of being thoroughly kissed.

J.M. glanced at the untouched coffee cups and the little plate of fancy cookies. "Uh, sorry to interrupt," he mumbled.

"You aren't interrupting, J.M. We were just having coffee," she said effusively. "Want some?"

Before he had time to answer, Brett muttered, "I'll get it," and disappeared into the kitchen.

J.M. tossed his hat onto the sofa. "Dammit, Annie, I should have called first. I just didn't think that you might be here."

"It's okay, J.M." She smiled warmly. "We're just neighbors." At the moment, she *knew* it was better this way. Maybe she was just looking for an excuse to leave tonight. That, she decided, was okay, too.

Brett returned with the coffeepot, filling a cup for his dad. J.M. didn't bother sitting, but took two cookies and drank his coffee while he paced around the room. His conversation was limited to stilted small talk spoken in brief sentences.

Brett watched his father move about, realizing that there was something else bothering him. Something besides a social visit and a discussion of the weather had brought him out here. "What is it? What's wrong?"

J.M. glanced quickly at Annie. "I guess I can speak confidentially in front of you, Annie. This isn't something I want spread around."

"Of course, J.M."

The sheriff looked at his son with a desperate appeal in his expression. "We've got to stop this profitable flow of illegals, Brett. We found an old van abandoned south of town this morning. It was locked. When we pried open the doors, we found six aliens. Two of them were dead from heat exhaustion and dehydration."

Annie gasped aloud. Was it possible that Carmen's husband . . . ? No, it was too horrible! She wouldn't allow herself to even consider such a pessimistic view. She had to believe that he would appear any day and that no ill had befallen him. "Who—do you know who they were?"

He shrugged. "We figure the men were here to work in the fields. We're still trying to identify them and notify families."

Men! She swallowed hard. "How . . . how old were they?"

J.M. studied the ceiling a moment. "I'd say they were in their fifties or older."

Annie felt somewhat relieved as she left Brett and his father that night. But J.M. had succeeded in planting a niggling fear in her heart.

6

A WEEK LATER Annie sat in the Jeep, staring at the mission ruins. An owl, eager for the approaching night, swept through the sky and landed on a distant tree. Her thoughts poured out as if in conversation.

What should I do about these women now? Do I let them stay? How can I turn them away? And what about Brett? He makes me feel wonderful and alive and special. We have the beginnings of what might be a good relationship. What would happen if he knew about them?

Her biggest worry was regarding Thomas, Carmen's husband. The poor girl checked daily to see if he'd arrived. But there was no sign of him, and the few immigrants who came through had no word of him. Sometimes Annie doubted if he even existed. Other times, she feared that he'd paid the ultimate price for freedom. And they had no way of knowing. Still, she couldn't send Isabel and Carmen off without him. In the back of her mind, she wondered what would happen if Thomas didn't come.

There were no answers to her pleading questions this particular evening. The ruins were perfectly quiet and still. She searched for signs of life, but the place appeared to be empty. After what Carmen had said about the ruins being a meeting place for refugees, though, she couldn't be certain that she was alone.

Feliz sat alert and attentive from the safety of the passenger seat beside Annie. The dog had curiously watched the owl and, at one point, growled at a touring coyote, but that was the extent of her guarding. She remained in the Jeep.

"You're no help," Annie grumbled softly, fondling the dog's ears. "All this time I thought you had extrasensory perception, and *los espíritus* kept you away. Now I see that you're afraid of strangers, whether alive or in spirit."

Feliz responded to Annie's voice by nuzzling her arm.

Annie stayed a while longer, trying to communicate with Aunt Annalee. But sitting in the Jeep just wasn't the same as walking among the ruins. There was a warmth in the bricks. Here, there were no special feelings. No whispered voices. No *ojos de los espíritus*.

With a heavy sigh, she started the engine.

The setting sun was painting the ancient adobe bricks a shade of brownish pink as she headed back to the house. When she arrived, she pulled in behind Brett's Mercedes. He was leaning casually against the door. A rush of excitement swept through her body, and her palms became sweaty.

Looking tanned and very handsome, Brett waited for her. His eyes were as dark as the approaching night and just as seductive. A slight smile softened his expression.

Annie tried to get a grip on her fluctuating emotions. He looked so incredibly appealing standing there, his arms folded across his broad chest. Everything about the man telegraphed strength. Along with dignity and scruples. And lawfulness. Annie felt just the opposite in his presence.

His voice was low and subdued. "Hey, Annie. How have you been this week?"

The woman in her responded with a warm inner vibrance and a smile. "Fine. And you?"

"The same. Busy."

She had missed him desperately this week. "Busy doing what?"

"Special assignment with the sheriff's department."

"Oh? What?"

"I'd rather not say. It's . . ."

"A secret?" she taunted.

"Something like that. How's the blossom-thinning going?" He was maddeningly evasive.

"Another week or so and we'll be finished."

He took her hands, feeling the palms and caressing them at the same time. "I've missed you, Annie."

"When I didn't hear from you, I thought you wouldn't be back."

"I couldn't stay away."

"I can't imagine why. Apple blossoms can't compete with the excitement of secret missions."

"I find being with you very exciting, Annie."

"Me? Exciting? That's a laugh. It's like watching apples grow."

His hands circled her wrists. She was sure he could feel her accelerated pulse, for it was raging inside her.

"To someone like me who's been overwhelmed with activity, watching apples grow can be enough. Something has lured me back here tonight when I could be . . . home."

"Or out on the town." She chuckled nervously.

"I'd rather be here with you, Annie." His voice was almost a whisper. "You hold the strongest attraction for me." He urged her closer so that she stood in the space between his widespread legs. "I want you, more than I ever believed possible."

"I'm flattered that such a man of the world would—"

"Find you alluring, captivating and enticing."

"Oh, Brett . . ." she scoffed, a little embarrassed by his choice of words. "Come on, now."

"The truth is, you're beautiful, Annie. And I'm . . ." he paused with a strained chuckle, "I hadn't exactly planned on this . . . this, uh, need to be near you. This desire to have you."

He pulled her against him and into his embrace. His lips found hers for a powerful, yearning kiss. At first she struggled against him, pushing on his chest, her body writhing and arching in a vain attempt to twist away. She feared that her strong attraction to him encouraged his eager aggression. How could it be right? They were so different—like night and day, black and white, *innocent and guilty.*

Persistently Brett held her, letting the kiss work its magic. As he tasted her sweet lips, a certain enchantment wove between them. For him, kissing her was bewitching, an act that was as irresistible as Annie herself. He didn't really understand her reluctance, for he detected her response and knew instinctively that it matched his.

At some point, a part of Annie's brain registered pleasure beyond belief, and she relaxed in his arms, succumbing to the weakness that invaded her limbs. His lips captured a small part of her in much the same way as his body seized her entire being. She was aware only of being engulfed in Brett's powerful maleness. And wanting more.

Then, suddenly, he released her. He ran his hand over his face. "Sorry, I lost it for a minute. You do that to me, whenever I'm near you. And sometimes, like now, I don't want to let go. I want you, Annie...."

She staggered back, feeling slightly dizzy, wanting to demand another, gentler kiss. But something in her fought for restraint. "Well, at least you're clear about your intentions," she murmured breathlessly.

"I've been with you a lot these past few weeks. But I knew immediately that I wanted you, wanted to make love to you, Annie. You knew, too...surely. You're not *that* naive. I thought it was what you wanted, too."

"Wait a minute!" She tucked her hair behind one ear. "Are you speaking for me? How do you know what I want? We haven't even discussed this."

He leaned forward and boldly caressed her lips with his. "Are you saying you don't want me to kiss you? Don't want me to hold you and make sweet, passionate love to you?"

She took a shaky breath. He wasn't playing fair. Just the sound of his sexy voice muttering those erotic words was enough to send her straight into his arms. "Oh, Brett, I don't know...."

"You've had this whole week to think it over."

"I didn't realize you'd given me a time limit."

"I'd hoped by now we'd—"

"How presumptuous of you!" She turned away from him and stood shivering with anger...or something she couldn't quite put her finger on.

"Don't pretend to be naive, Annie." Standing behind her, he placed his hands on her shoulders, then slid them down her arms so that he eventually embraced her from behind. "This attraction we have is mutual, so don't deny it."

His arms felt strong around her, and that strength relayed security. She calmed down, finally admitting, "Yes, I'm attracted to you, Brett. Who wouldn't be?"

Tightening his embrace, he pulled her against him. "You know it's special. You can feel the vibes between us, whether we're touching or not."

Annie felt more than vibes. His body was strong and hard and reaching out for her. And she wanted desperately to yield to him. But there was more at stake than one feverish night. She tried to ignore the appeal his body had for hers.

His voice rumbled low. "Annie, you've known all along that I wanted you."

She flared. "And that's why you're here tonight? For a a . . . quick romp?"

He took a ragged breath. Dammit, she was trying her darnedest to make him angry. Determinedly he refused. He would muddle through her resistance and prove that he cared for more than her body. But right now, as passion raged through him, it was difficult. He forced an unnatural calmness to his voice. "I came here to see how you feel about it, that's all."

"Doesn't anybody ever ask anymore?" Even as Annie lashed out at him, she sensed she was manifesting a battle that existed only within herself. She wanted to fight these feelings, to resist him. But she also wanted him.

"Okay, I'm asking," he said quietly. "Don't you feel the same as I do? Don't you want me like crazy, Annie? Tell me no, and I'll leave."

"I . . ." She placed her hands over his and felt the chill of the night sweep over them. He was putting everything on the line and demanding that she make a decision *now*. "Dammit, Brett! I don't know."

He sighed heavily, and she knew she was testing his patience. But she'd been so confused lately, doing things she'd never done before—like harboring refugees. Like letting her feelings for Brett run rampant. Her logic said *Don't get involved with him*. But her heart said *Don't let this moment slip away*.

"I think you do know, you just don't want to admit it. Let's go inside and discuss this like two rational adults."

"Or two passionate adults?"

He hesitated. Did he detect a lightness, a flicker of a possibility to her voice? He could only be honest with her, and hope. "Passion is normal between adults. It isn't bad, Annie. We can just see if it'll work out. If not, no hard feelings." He stopped short of predicting what would happen if things did work out between them.

"Maybe . . . maybe that's not such a bad idea, Brett."

Clasping hands, they entered the dark house together. They moved through the kitchen and dining room, then paused in the living room. The house was silent and dimly lit. They were alone. Both were calmer now. Brett helped to remove her jacket, lightly caressing her shoulders and arms in the process.

Annie returned the gesture, letting her hands trail down the muscular length of his arms. They stood facing each other in the shadowed evening light, fingers loosely hooked together.

"Should we turn on a lamp and discuss the situation?" she asked after a few moments.

"I'd rather let the night persuade us." He kissed her fingertips with lips warm and tender. Then his mouth claimed hers. As the kiss slowly deepened and grew in strength and fervor, his hands moved up her arms to grip her shoulders and haul her against him. He felt her body come willingly to his, her delicate frame conforming to his solid structure.

Her breasts pushed against him, creating a quickening in his muscular chest and a turbulence below his waist. He wrapped his arms around her back, fingers spread to encompass all of her or as much as he could touch. He was so filled with desire for her that he wanted, momentarily, to crush her to him.

Annie met his kiss with no resistance. Weak and willing in his arms, she opened her mouth to his, accepting his sweet, hard tongue. Never had she felt so submissive, and yet she felt strangely aggressive at the same time. Something in her demanded that if he didn't take charge of the situation, she would.

The commotion within her breast spread through her entire being... a swirling, growing, pulsing desire. Moaning softly, Annie writhed against him, feeling him with her body, imagining his flesh next to hers. Her halfhearted resistance of only a few minutes ago was gone. The moment was all that mattered. She didn't care if Brett left tomorrow, she wanted him tonight.

His lips made a moist trail down her neck to the glen between her breasts. She took a shaky breath and leaned her head back to invite and enjoy every teasing foray of his tantalizing tongue.

"Annie . . . Annie . . . so sweet," he murmured beneath her earlobe.

"I think you've already made up your mind, Brett." She straightened, trying not to show her breathlessness. "And are intent on making up mine."

"I decided long ago." His hands cupped and lifted her breasts while his thumbs stroked the tips through her sweater. "I want to kiss these, kiss them until you beg me to stop. And I want to show you the pleasures of a complete and total body massage." His hand moved to her groin, caressing through her clothes. "And I want to know every inch of you . . ."

His words were erotic. His touch was arousing. She was hot beneath the constant stroking of his hand; she thought she'd burst for wanting him and arched against the pressure of his fingers. "Brett. . . ."

"Ah, Annie, don't keep me waiting any longer. Or you." He shifted so that his arousal prodded her belly. "You want every inch of me, don't you?"

"Yes . . ." Drunk from the wine of his kisses, she clung to him, forgetting all her doubts and dubious reasons for resisting the magnificent man who claimed to want her. "Oh, yes! Take me, Brett."

In one sweeping motion, he lifted her into his arms and headed down the hall. "Where's your bedroom?"

"Last door on the left," she murmured against his neck.

He stood her next to the bed. "Are you prepared with birth control, Annie?"

"No, I—"

"Then I'll take care of it."

He moved away from her, and she strained in the darkness to watch him undress. She could see only his dark outline, but that was erotic enough to send pulsing jets of passion surging through her body.

After shedding his own clothes, Brett returned to her, his hands and lips caressing every newly exposed feminine curve. In an almost desperate eagerness, they came together on the bed, a writhing ensemble of dark and light. His large tanned body dominated hers, while her fair-haired beauty lured him into submission.

Hands touched, exploring. Lips cooed and moaned softly. Gentle giggles punctuated the otherwise quiet night. Annie thought she might be in heaven when she sank into Brett's arms. And when he kissed her, she *knew* she was.

His lips traced the pale curves of her breasts, closing over each dark and distended nipple, tugging on the tight buds. Swelling from within, Annie wanted to thrust her aching breasts fully into his mouth.

Then, leaving her wanting more, he kissed his way down her rib cage and over the angle of her hipbone. He kissed a path along each tender inner thigh, creating a continuum of wild desire that reverberated through her like a bass drum, throbbing and pounding and demanding to be fulfilled.

But when his tongue drew a hot liquid line through the center of her femininity, Annie arched and groaned aloud, clutching fiercely at his shoulders.

"Please..." she begged.

"What? What do you want?" He touched her again, stroking, caressing, driving himself crazy in the process. He thought he would burst if he didn't hurry. "Tell me," he demanded raggedly.

"You." Her voice was no more than a hoarse gasp. "I want you, Brett."

"Oh, yes, my beautiful, sweet Annie." He slid up her body and settled between her legs. The power of his engorged manhood pressed against her, then into her, merging their bodies. The sexual energy flowed back and forth until they were one, striving toward the same climax. He tried to pace himself, but he could feel the crescendo building inside him until he lost contact with reality. He moved vigorously, an instrument of power and strength, plunging into her with no control.

Brett lifted her hips and drove further, feeling stronger and more alive than he had in months. Annie was here for him; she was his. She was the one he had been waiting for all these years.

Annie found his power exciting. He filled her with passions long denied, and her body sang in harmony with his. When they merged, they blended beautifully in a duet of desire that quickly swelled to a triumphant jubilation. She had never experienced such fulfillment.

Brett was a special man, and tonight he was hers. He felt exactly right in her arms. Her happiness was complete.

The finale came with a flurry of movements and loud cymbals, taking them both to the pinnacle. He exploded with strength and rage, and she wrapped her arms around his middle and held on.

For Annie, the peak was equally intense and satisfying. And Brett held her tightly, experiencing the ecstasy with her. For the first time in his life he felt satisfaction with his lover's climax. And when she finally relaxed beneath him, he cradled her against his chest. They dozed off together.

Sometime later, he stirred and tried to slip away.

Instinctively Annie clutched him. "Brett, don't leave."

He sighed and lay back on the pillow. "Annie...I probably should go."

Bracing her forearms on his chest, she leaned over and kissed the sleek muscles. "Please stay, Brett. I want to wake up in your arms."

"All night? Are you sure?"

"Yes." She rested her head on his chest and gently stroked his side, feeling the ridge of the horrible scar beneath her fingertips. "I'm not ready to let you go yet."

With a grateful groan, he turned to embrace her, nestling them together like two spoons. "Well, I certainly don't want to leave you."

Relaxing, drifting, they shifted again, finding comfortable positions for the night's sleep, bodies nudging, arms reaching out, legs crossing. Annie felt the security of another person for the first time since she had moved to the apple farm. She leaned against his solid chest and slept deeply.

Brett pulled her warm, slender body to his and slept through the night. For the first time since the shooting, he didn't wake to a nightmare.

He rose early, slipping out of bed, still nude, to fix coffee. Annie would like that, he reasoned.

It was much later, when sunlight was streaming through the window across the bed, that Annie finally stirred. She nuzzled his arm with her face and began to smile even before her eyes opened to engulf him in their verdant happiness. Her skin was pale and her form was delicate beside his large brown body. An endearing morning-after love blush tinted her cheeks, and he watched her stretch and yawn as long as he could without touching her.

Then he wrapped her in his arms and kissed her until, sputtering and laughing, she pushed him away. "Please! Let me get my breath! You certainly wake up eager and energetic."

"That's not all," he warned with a teasing growl, swinging one of his legs over hers. "Would you like to know how energetic I can be? How about a little horizontal aerobics?"

Laughing, she sniffed the air. "Did you make coffee already?"

"It's my best dish, remember?"

"Oh, you dear, wonderful man, anticipating my every need." She lay back on the pillow and looked up at him with an admiring smile. "How very sweet. And you came back to bed so I'd wake up so gloriously in your arms?"

Lovingly he spread her strawberry hair across the pillow, then slid his hand beneath her neck. His eyes narrowed and his voice took on admonishing tone. "It was amazing to learn that when you're asleep, you don't care who you cuddle up to."

"Oh, you—" She lunged for him and after a brief, squealing tussle, ended up on her back with her hands pinned beside her head.

Brett hovered over her. "You can't deny you tempted me, even in your sleep."

"*Por favor, capitan, yo inocente!*" she claimed in her poor Spanish. "I didn't know what I was doing."

"Innocent? I don't buy that." He kissed her hard, then looked at her with heavy-lidded eyes. "You're incorrigible. And incredible. It was all I could do to resist ravaging your body this morning while you were asleep."

"You wouldn't! Oh! You devil!" She tried to struggle out of his grasp, but he held her securely and kissed her again.

Submitting to his overpowering grasp, she sighed. "I thought you were going to deliver my coffee to bed," she murmured in a sexy whisper.

"Would you like that?" He released her hands and trailed one finger down her nose, chin and neck. The trail then strayed to one breast and slowly circled the tip.

"Hmm," she moaned. "Nice. Yes, I would love to have coffee in bed."

He kissed her nose. "Can't resist such a polite lady. Can't stand the begging in those cat eyes of yours. And I can't possibly lie here next to that luscious body of yours without wanting it. So I may as well get the coffee."

As he scooted away from her, the sheet dropped below his waist, revealing the ugly scar. Annie reached out to gently caress it. "Does it hurt?"

"No."

"You have such a strong, tough body. A nice body. . ."

"Now that little-known fact has been discovered by more than one female around this house." He stepped into his jeans and pulled them over his lean hips. "Why didn't you tell me someone else lived here?"

"What do you mean? No one else lives here. Only Diego out back."

He gazed at her steadily. "Annie, an older woman, looked to be Mexican, came into the kitchen this morning as I was fixing coffee. Now, you're telling me you don't know who she is?"

Annie gasped. "Oh, no!"

"Oh, yes. Then you know her?"

She nodded mutely, feeling absolutely trapped.

"Thank goodness." Brett chuckled, his dark eyes dancing. "I don't know who was more surprised, me or the woman."

Annie figured Isabel had probably been shocked. She sat up in bed, pulling the sheet to her breasts. "What did you do?"

"I said good morning."

"Were you . . ." She motioned to his body.

"Completely." He grinned. "I'd say she got a full view of my bare buns, but disappeared before—"

"Brett!"

"It livened up the morning. I just wish you'd warned me." He paused by the door. "Or her. I think she was pretty astonished. She disappeared without even returning my greeting."

Annie slapped her forehead and slumped down in bed with a groan. She had forgotten about giving Isabel and Carmen permission to fix breakfast, since they both needed a more nutritious diet. But, at the time, she hadn't anticipated that Brett would be here.

When he returned with two cups of coffee, she apologized and tried to explain, telling him as little as possible about woman.

Much to her relief, Brett was unconcerned about the reasons. "You don't have to apologize to me for what happens in your house, Annie. I'm just an overnight guest." He settled beside her, stretching his jean-clad legs on top of the covers. "But I would like to be invited back."

"You should know you have a standing invitation. Or—" she grinned "—a lying-in invitation, as the case may be."

"Is that an offer for a repeat performance?"

"Maybe..." She sipped her hot coffee. "Ahh, this is great."

"I want you to know, Annie, that you're the best thing that's happened to me in a long, long time."

"I'm flattered, Brett. I'm not exciting, though. I lead an ordinary, quiet life."

"That's part of what I like, I think. You're honest. And steady. And good."

"Oh, come on now." She hooted and gestured above her head. "Do you see a halo? Or wings?"

"Compared to most of the women I've known, you're like a little jewel."

"Brett, you're embarrassing me. You don't even know me. Not really."

"Last night didn't tell?"

She smiled secretively. "Not the whole story."

"I know enough," he said confidently. Setting their empty cups on the night table, he turned to her, framing her oval face with his large hands. His kisses praised her cheeks and chin and lips. "Did I ever tell you that you're beautiful?"

She grinned and shook her head. "Not in the last five minutes."

"Well, then, you're beautiful." The kiss that followed was long and moist and left no doubt about the way he felt right now: passionate, and turned-on.

She touched his face with gentle stroking fingers. "You're beautiful, too, Brett."

Before long she was helping him remove his jeans and enticing him to make love again. This time they went slowly in the morning light, sharing and giving and exploring instead of feverishly clamoring in the dark. Their eagerly reached ecstasy was as glorious as the sunrise.

After they had showered, Annie wrapped herself in a towel and sat on the bed, watching Brett dress.

His bare body was lean and hard and darkly tanned. The one flaw on his entire gorgeous physique was the ugly scar beneath his ribs. Otherwise he was perfect. And perfect for her. More than perfect.

"Very nice," she cooed as he slid the jeans on and buttoned his shirt. His jeans were still creased, even though they had been tossed on a chair overnight. And his boots were shiny. He was the same immaculate man who had first arrived a few weeks ago.

"Would you like to stay for breakfast? It's not my best meal, but I'm sure I could rustle up something."

"No. I'd better go. We both have to work today." He zipped his jeans and gave her a meaningful glance. "That doesn't mean I wouldn't like to stay. I just think we'd better take it easy."

She nodded. "Right."

He walked over to where she sat on the bed and bent to kiss her quickly. "What we have is a good thing, Annie. Let's not spoil it."

"Sure." Annie felt a sudden sadness, knowing he was leaving.

"I'll be back."

"Anytime."

He kissed her quickly and was gone.

She sat unmoving on the bed, listening to his rapidly retreating footsteps in the hall. Why did she feel so empty? Because he was gone? Or because of a sense of guilt for deceiving him?

What troubled her was that Brett had unreal expectations of her. He thought she was—he had used the word *innocent*. But she wasn't!

And yet, she had no intention of changing. She had made a commitment to Isabel and Carmen to see them through their immediate problems and on their way. And she could not break her word, even if it meant continuing to break the law.

She knew she should tell Brett about the people taking refuge on her farm, before things went any further between them. Before he placed her on this unrealistic pedestal, she had to tell him the truth. And she definitely would tell him . . . soon.

Annie glanced at the clock and hurriedly dressed. As Brett said, there was work to do today. She searched for her boots, finally finding them on the back porch—caked with mud. Inspired by Brett's example, she tossed them onto an old newspaper and began scrubbing furiously.

7

SHE HAD TO TELL HIM. The guilt was driving her crazy.

This was what happened to people who were so honest they squeaked, Annie thought as she drove to Brett's place on Saturday. She'd committed one *little* transgression and was plagued with guilt.

Charged with the urge to confess, Annie clutched a grocery bag and knocked on his front door. Brett greeted her, dressed in cutoff jeans and an old gray sweatshirt with sleeves trimmed unevenly above the elbows. She was amazed that even in this ragged attire, he looked neat and devastatingly handsome.

Smiling, he breathed her name and welcomed her with a kiss. "Annie, what a beautiful surprise."

"Did I catch you at a bad time?"

"Naw, just busy. But never too busy for you." He stepped back. "Come on and see what I'm doing."

She gazed around the nearly empty living room. "Where's all the furniture?"

"J.M. took it yesterday." He gestured at the kitchen stool in the middle of the room. "Have a seat while I finish this wall before my plaster dries. I'm patching the walls, getting ready to paint."

Annie perched on the step stool and watched him work, an appreciative grin on her face. The sight of Brett stretching and bending and reaching was so pleasurable that she just sat there, enjoying the view for a few minutes. Finally she asked, "So, did J.M. decide to rescue the furniture when you told him you didn't want it?"

"Would you believe he's been living in a furnished rental all this time?"

"Why?"

"I don't know. Didn't want to disturb the old homestead, I guess. Probably too many reminders around here."

"He must have loved your mother very much," she observed in a quiet voice.

"Yeah, and you want to know something funny? When I was a kid, I didn't believe he loved anyone. He was too gruff and demanding. What I didn't realize was that he was preoccupied with constant financial problems, always on the verge of bankruptcy and losing the ranch. With that kind of stress, he found it difficult to show his love."

"But he sent you to that private military school. And on to college. How could he afford to do that?"

"It didn't cost him anything. My maternal grandfather set up a trust fund for me when I was born." Brett propped one foot on the raised tile hearth around the beehive fireplace and leaned an elbow on his knee. "My mother's family was quite wealthy."

"You were lucky. The best my folks could do was to send me here, to Aunt Annalee and Uncle Martin, for the summers. The country life was my education."

"Funny, isn't it?" Brett examined the ceiling, then stretched to patch the flaws he noticed. "Your folks sent you here. Mine sent me away. My dad didn't see the ranch as any kind of future for me."

"Do you?"

"Maybe." He nodded with satisfaction and made a final stroke above his head. "I understand now that part of the problem my dad had with this place was that he and my mother inherited it from her grandfather, who had received this property in a Spanish land grant."

"So it had been in her family for many years?"

"Right. And when they moved here as newlyweds, the expectation was that J.M. would continue to make the ranch profitable with horses and cattle. And he tried. He really did. Trouble was, he wasn't much of a rancher. He was never interested in breeding cattle, nor was he very good with horses." Brett finished the fireplace and closed the plaster container. "But if Dad, or any of the area ranchers, had trouble with poachers or rustlers, he was the first one there to help solve the crime. I remember once when he left for two weeks to join a posse that trailed a bunch of rustlers into Colorado."

"So, as sheriff, J.M.'s finally doing what he loves?"

"Yep. I believe that a lawman is exactly what he was meant to be. He's damn good at his job. Now that I'm working with him, I see how thorough and diligent he is. And, believe it or not, he's a caring man. He's just gruff on the outside."

"Like father, like son."

"Yep, in a lot of ways, I guess." Brett grinned sheepishly. "I do love to solve a crime or make a case on a criminal. But I also share some of my Hispanic ancestors' satisfaction in making a living by the sweat of my brow. Take this work, for instance." He motioned to the freshly plastered walls. "This has been a great project for me. I really enjoy working with my hands and seeing a finished product."

"So do I," Annie agreed. "That's why I'm growing apples instead of counting other people's money. You know, you should have called me today. I told you I'd help. Anyway, I owe you a couple of days' labor, at least."

"You owe me nothing, Annie. Anyway, I knew you were still busy thinning your blossoms."

"I'll bet J.M. is delighted that you're fixing up the old place."

"He's pleased. It means I'm staying for a while."

"Then I'm pleased, too."

Brett's dark eyes danced, and he glanced at the bag she held. "What'cha got? Lunch?"

She grinned slyly. "You could say that." Slowly she began to reveal the bag's contents.

"Ah, *vino*, nectar of the gods," he said in a melodic voice.

"No. It's berry wine coolers," she corrected. "Just as good, only less alcohol."

"Berry cool coolers," he quipped as she continued to pull out each item and set it on the hearth beside him. "And bread, the staff of life. All right! Cheese, the ancient sustenance. You sure know the right foods for a perfect afternoon." He grabbed her and pulled her into his arms for a quick kiss. "What a generous and lovely neighbor you are."

"What a starving and receptive neighbor *you* are," she returned with a giggle.

He took a seat on the hearth and tumbled her into his lap. "Manners dictate that I kiss you good 'n' proper, to show my appreciation, of course."

"Of course." She was laughing as his lips captured hers. Her heart soared with the warmth of his reception. He could be so playful, and yet she sometimes forgot that in the face of his seriousness.

"Oh, yes, Annie . . ." he said as the kiss began to work its sensual magic on them both. "There's only one place to do this right." He thrust the long loaf of bread into her arms and picked up the wine cooler four-pack and cheese.

"What? Where?"

"We'll have a picnic." He ushered her into his old bedroom. "A bed picnic!"

"Oh, no, Brett," she resisted. "I don't want to disturb your work."

"You disturbed more than my work when you walked in that door, my dear." He dropped his items onto the bed. "Anyway, I'm finished with my work for the day. Don't want to overdo it. That'll leave nothing for tomorrow."

She looked at the single twin bed with its brightly colored Mexican blanket. "But, Brett, this is a . . . kid's room."

"Not anymore." He took the bread from her and tossed it onto the bed, too. Then he placed breathy kisses on her lips and along her jawline and beneath her earlobe. "This is a place for a man and woman. I'll be right back with a knife for the cheese."

Annie gazed at the bed strewn with their picnic items. She could hear Brett scrambling in a kitchen drawer. And then she remembered her mission. She'd completely forgotten her confession!

Sighing, she grabbed one of the wine coolers, opened it and took a long drink. Nothing was going the way she had planned. Her intention was to soften the mood for her thunderbolt, not create a sensuous scene. But Brett had other ideas. She couldn't really blame him. She shouldn't have brought wine coolers and cheese and crusty French bread. She should have brought soda and pretzels and a paintbrush.

Brett returned in a minute, brandishing a wooden-handled paring knife. He paused to kiss her cheek. "This old thing probably won't cut hot butter," he murmured. "I'll do my best carve a wedge of cheddar... you hunk-off the bread." He sat Indian style on the bed and tossed her the bread.

"Hunk-off?" She laughed giddily. "Is that a real word? I think you made it up." She sat opposite him, trying to figure out how to bring up the sensitive subject without spoiling the mood.

"You get the picture, don't you?"

"Indeed, yes." She ripped into the foil bag and tore off a section of bread.

"Yeah, you've got the idea."

Annie looked at him, feeling miserable inside. He was in such good spirits, how could she spoil their fun? She could tell him later. What was the rush, anyway? Oh, she was a first-class, royal chicken! She took a bite of the bread and gave him one.

He grinned and fed her a thin slice of cheddar.

She poked another piece of chewy fresh bread into his mouth.

He slipped a sliver of cheese between her lips.

She put the wine cooler bottle to his lips for a drink.

Either he shifted or she slipped, but she splashed berry wine cooler down his chin. That simple little accident started it.

He yelled and lunged for her. She squealed and jumped, spilling the cooler on herself, too. Laughing, he playfully took her down. By the time the scuffle was over, Annie was on her back on the Mexican blanket. Brett was kissing her to distraction and, Annie was kissing him back.

Any guilty feelings she'd had slipped clear out of her mind when his tongue edged her lips. Nothing else mattered except opening for more pleasure. And when his hand pressed her breast in a gentle massage, she completely forgot her reason for coming over here in the first place.

She had learned, in the past few weeks, that when Brett labored, she could watch those muscles flex all day long. When he laughed, she could drown in his deep, dark eyes. But when he kissed her, well, she was driven to abandon all reason.

He squeezed one of his hands between them to unsnap her jeans. Her zipper slid open. Pinned beneath his strong body, she waited, knowing that he would come feeling for her. Slowly, ever so slowly, his hand inched down her belly, sliding inside her silk panties. Her flesh tingled with fire. Her blood turned to steam as he caressed sensitive areas. Her feminine center became soft and moist as he stroked with firm mastery.

Annie didn't know how she could possibly want anyone as much as she did Brett at this moment.

Brett raised his head and propped himself on one elbow to watch her vibrant reactions to his touch. In their titillating roughhousing, her ponytail had come undone and now her hair streamed like flames about her head on the Mexican blanket. Her eyes were closed, thick sorrel lashes feathering her pale cheeks. Her sensuous crimson lips parted slightly, allowing sharp little breaths to escape through her mouth. Unable to resist her another moment, Brett bent to mingle his breath with hers.

Watching her responses had been such a turn-on, he feared he would explode before they even had time to get undressed. As she moaned and arched against his hand, he realized that right now, strange as it seemed, her pleasure was all that mattered to him.

He had never really cared much about his partner's responses before Annie. Oh, he had wanted to know that his woman was satisfied, but to think of her needs alone, unselfishly excluding his, had never occurred to him. Until now. Until Annie.

"Hey, pretty girl . . ."

Her eyes popped open, and she knew that he had been watching her. She didn't care. She wanted him to know how she felt. "Oh, Brett, I can't stand this much longer."

"Me, either." He withdrew his hand from her blue jeans and began to undress her. "I want you, Annie."

"Here?" Although she questioned him, she helped him discard her clothes. "In your . . . this room?"

"I think it's time we christened this as an adult room. After all, I certainly spent enough time dreaming of taking a beautiful, sexy woman to my bed when I was a teen." He skinned his shirt over his head. "Course I could never dream of someone as incredible as you."

"I'll bet!" She laughed with glee as she tugged his shorts off his hips to reveal him in all his aroused, masculine glory. "All right," she murmured as she sank down on the blanket. "Tell the truth. Did you ever bring anyone here, Brett?"

His eyes were like two glowing coals, dark and on fire. "No, Annie. You're the only one. This is a special place. And you..." He moved to her side. "You're a special woman. My special woman..."

"I like that," she murmured.

He kissed one sensitive, swollen breast until the tip puckered tightly in his lips, then moved to the other. "You are the bright spot in my life, Annie." He kissed her lips, teasing the corners with his tongue. "You are beautiful and smart and sweetly innocent. You're everything I need in a woman. Everything I want."

He had used that word again. *Innocent.* She was guilty as sin, but now was definitely not the time to tell him. She would do it later.

She touched his chest, caressing every muscle as her hand blazed a heated trail to his waist, then further down. "And you're the kind of strong, sensitive man I've always hoped to know. To love."

He kissed her cheeks and chin and the column of her neck. Then he moved back to her lips and found them open for him. "Loving you is fabulous, Annie. You're so very sweet. I want you all the time."

With growing bravado, she stroked the hard, quivering male flesh beneath her hand. "I wish I could believe you'll never leave, Brett."

"I'll always be here for you, Annie." His voice became strained as she helped him make their loving safe. "I swear..."

She closed her hand tightly over him. "You'd swear to anything right now."

He groaned and lay back. "You're right," he muttered with a low chuckle. "I'm yours. Now and forever. To do with whatever you will."

Taking his challenge, she rolled over him, straddling his large body with pale, slender legs. Grabbing his wrists, she pretended to pin him as he had done to her. "I'm going to love you until you beg me to stop. And then—" She ground her pelvis against him. "We're going another round."

He grinned up at her. "You sound rough for such a skinny little paleface."

"Skinny!" She flattened herself against him, kissing him until they were breathless. Raising her hips, she came down upon him, merging them slowly and completely. The passionate minutes stretched out into eternity as the ageless, familiar rhythm encompassed them, taking them beyond reality to the nebulous realm of total and glorious rapture.

After a considerable time, Annie floated from a half-conscious stupor back to conscious reality. As the sensuous throbbing of her body slowed, she thought of her mission. She had come here to talk with Brett about something very important. Instead, they had made love. How could she have succumbed to this?

Brett shifted under her, and she remembered that *she* was in the position of power. With chagrin, she knew that she wasn't blameless here. She had seduced him, as well. Her emotions were reeling along with her reason. Unfortunately, she could not resist his magnificent male charm. As Annie lay over him, she knew without a doubt that she had fallen for more than his sexual charms.

With a flush of heat that rushed through her whole body, she realized that she had slipped into love with Brett. And that was a foolish and risky thing to do.

But this ill-fated love she felt was the reason that she wanted to come clean about her crimes. Not only was confession good for the soul, it cleansed the heart and conscience, too. Only, in this case, it might ruin a lovely relationship. And break a heart. Maybe she should just keep her secret.

He stirred beneath her. "Annie...it's shower time. I'm great at back scrubbing."

"Sounds wonderful." She raised up and looked down into those gorgeous brown eyes of his. How could she be anything less than completely and totally honest with him? She had to tell him—right after the shower. She rolled off him.

He caressed her bare bottom as he followed her down the hall to the bathroom. "You're a great little lover, you know that?"

"You aren't so bad, yourself."

"I continually find you surprising."

"Oh? How?"

"Well, I used to think of you as the skinny kid next door. But now I realize you're one of the most amazing women I've ever known." He adjusted the shower. "And every time we make love, you convince me again to stick around."

"And all this time I thought you were here to chase criminals."

"Only half the night. The rest is saved for you."

She looked surprised. "Is that what you did last night?"

He disappeared behind the shower curtain. "Every night."

Later, wrapped in a towel, she pursued the conversation further. "Is that where you go when you leave me at night? Out looking for criminals?"

"Or waiting for them."

Annie felt sick. She remembered what J.M. had said about stopping the traffic of aliens. "Are you talking about the smugglers?"

Brett opened one of the wine coolers and took a swig. "My job is to try to apprehend them and break the chain."

"That's your special assignment with the sheriff's department?" she asked weakly. "Your secret mission?"

"Look, Annie, I'm sure I don't need to tell you to keep all this quiet."

"Of course not. I won't breathe a word to anyone."

"My goal is to make a dent in the ability of these jerks to profit from poor people's misfortune and an ignorance of our system. Ultimately I want to put a stop to the heavy flow of illegals into this country through our borders."

Annie listened mesmerized. She could see Brett's enthusiasm grow as he talked about his project. And every word filled her with more guilt and misery. It was quite apparent that he loved his job. Obviously he thought he could trust her.

He frowned and studied her expression. "Are you okay, Annie? You aren't disturbed by all this talk about criminals, are you?"

"Of course not," she lied. "Just a little...amazed." That part was true.

"Most of the general public have no idea what kinds of crime are going on all around them."

Annie took a bite of bread, but it stuck in her dry mouth. She knew she couldn't tell him today. Not now. Oh, Lord, she was getting in deeper.

"Sometimes even the most seemingly innocent..." he was saying.

8

ANNIE WALKED into the mayor's office and gazed around. "I see your air conditioner's still working, Lacy. And your plants are still growing."

Lacy poured them each a glass of iced tea and topped the drink with a sprig of mint. "I have you to thank for donating the air conditioner. And my office plants are doing okay. But I must be losing my touch with the ones in the garden at home. Several have turned yellow and died in the past few weeks." She handed Annie the tea. "I've never had this kind of trouble before."

Annie grinned. "Let's see now. You have three kids and a cat and dog with this newly acquired family?"

"Three kids, *two* cats, a dog and a husband."

"And a town," Annie reminded her.

"Right."

"Well, I'd say that's your reason."

"Neglect?" Lacy sat in a side chair and motioned for Annie to take the opposite seat. It was a cosy corner for chatting and eliminated the barrier of the mayor's large desk.

"No, the animals. Are you sure they aren't wandering among the plants, doing . . . their *business*?"

Lacy chuckled. "Well, they certainly aren't supposed to. But I'll have a word with the kids about that." Lacy frowned. "Maybe, to be safe, I'd better fence in my plants and let the animals and kids run free."

"Good idea. Those plants aren't going anywhere."

"How are things with you, Annie? Did the late frost do much damage?"

"Most of the blossoms survived." Annie held up two crossed fingers. "And it looks like I'm going to have a decent crop."

"Profitable?"

"I don't want to count my apples too soon, but, maybe."

"Good. Is there anything we can do to help?"

"I don't know of anything."

"Help you hire workers?"

Annie tried to keep her reaction casual, but the *last* thing she wanted was additional people around the farm right now. Her refugees would bring scandal to everyone, including her friend, the mayor. And she certainly didn't want that. "Diego and I have things under control, thanks. There isn't much to do now except keep them watered and watch them grow. Oh, yes, and watch for thrips."

"What's thrips?"

"A little bug that occurs in the early-apple stage. It bites under the skin and leaves that little brown spot you sometimes see on apple skins. It's more unsightly than harmful but makes them quite unmarketable."

"Well, we certainly don't want that," Lacy said. Tentatively she broached another subject. "I understand you've had a little help from your neighbor."

"If you mean Brett, yes, he's been very helpful."

Lacy waited for more elaboration on the helpful neighbor, but Annie wasn't talking. "Well, that's what neighbors are for. I'm glad to see you working together."

Annie wasn't about to reveal just how closely she and Brett had been working together. She wasn't comfortable enough with their relationship at this point; the whole thing seemed to be hanging by a thread. And if Brett found out about her refugees, that thread might just snap.

"You mentioned a new project you wanted to discuss with me, Lacy. That's why I stopped by on my way to get supplies."

Lacy smiled gently as Annie diverted the conversation from Brett. "Right. This is something I'm very excited about, and I hope you will be, too. Holt says the building we're going to use for the museum will be ready in a few months. With a little good input and inspiration from someone like you, Annie, I think the committee could have it open in time for the autumn fiesta."

"More work, you mean," Annie drawled.

"Yes, that, too." Lacy produced a typed document. "Here, this'll explain the goals of the museum committee so far."

Annie dug into her purse for her glasses, then scanned the papers. "But, Lacy, I don't know anything about history and the early pioneers' lives."

"You don't have to. We have plenty of history buffs for that. What I'd like for you to contribute is some creative ideas for the displays. But also, I'd like to dedicate at least one room of the museum to folk arts. You know, the things that gave the settlers pleasure and entertainment."

"You mean, what they did in their spare time without TV?"

"Exactly."

"Lacy, they had no spare time. They worked from daylight to dark, just to exist."

"That isn't true, Annie. Think about it. They were people, just like us, who worked and worried, but also had fun, too." She lifted her glass for emphasis. "Just as my hobby is growing and cooking with herbs, they had hobbies, too. What were they? And, can we find any good examples?"

"You mean arts and crafts? Wood carving and knitting and stuff like that?"

"Yes." Lacy nodded. "But the people who settled here had some different ones, too."

Annie wrinkled her nose. "Rag dolls and aprons? Like they have in Grannie's Attic, the new shop that sells handmade items?"

Lacy leaned forward enthusiastically. "How about some of the things that were unique to the Southwest, like clay dolls? And tin art? Our culture includes not only the Anglos who settled, but the Spanish, German, Polish and Chinese who immigrated here. And the original Native Americans and Mexicans who were here first. What kinds of skills did they bring to enrich their lives? Those things make up our heritage."

"I see. You want me to look into the cultural heritage." Annie pondered the proposal for a minute. "Okay, sounds interesting." She pulled out a pen and began taking notes on their discussion.

"I'm glad you think so, Annie. I'd like to see the folk arts display turn into something special, a rare look at the skills and crafts of those who passed through this land before us. I hoped you'd agree. Some of these skills might be dying arts and are worthy of being preserved."

Annie thought of those people who were passing through her farm on their way to a new life. They were, she supposed, a lot like the early pioneers who left homelands and struck out into the unknown, looking for a better life.

Isabel hadn't felt well for several days, probably from working too hard helping with the blossom thinning. And Carmen was getting more and more anxious about Thomas. She was growing bigger daily and, even with her thinness and loose clothing, she was no longer able to hide her pregnancy.

Lacy's voice intruded. "Don't you agree? Annie?"

"Huh? Oh, yes, Lacy. I agree. Sounds interesting. I'll see what I can find for the museum."

"Great. Does that mean you'll join the committee? They really need you."

Annie paused, but the enthusiasm Lacy sparked for a project made it difficult to tell her no. "Sure. When do they meet?"

"Tomorrow night, seven o'clock, at the old office across the hall."

"Who's on the committee?"

Lacy ticked them off on her fingers. "Let's see. Holt's the chairman. Then there's Maxine. And, uh, Vinnie. She doesn't come regularly, but she contributes during other times."

"That's all? Two regulars?"

"Three, with you. And I'm working on the librarian, who could provide some of the research. That would make four." Lacy studied her tea glass. "Of course, we could use more members. Maybe you know someone who would like to contribute a small part of his time for a very worthwhile endeavor?"

"*His* time? Are you hinting at anyone specific, Mayor?"

Lacy pursed her lips. "We really need someone who's smart and interested in preserving Silverton and who has a direct link to a vital segment of our history. Maybe even someone with Hispanic ancestors."

"Someone tall, dark and handsome?"

"Wouldn't hurt. Know anyone who fits that description?"

"How about Diego?"

Lacy shook her head, her blue eyes dancing. "He isn't tall."

Annie burst out laughing. "You aren't being very subtle, Lacy."

"I know. But Brett is a natural for this."

"I don't even know if he's interested in our history."

"Why, Annie, of course he is. He talked at length with Holt about how to fix up his old homestead. Did you know that part of that house existed from the Spanish land grant days? Now, why would he bother with that if he didn't care?"

"He . . . wouldn't, I guess," Annie muttered thoughtfully. "Well, I can ask and see if he'll join us."

Lacy smiled happily. "I knew you would. You always have such a willing attitude, Annie. Thanks."

"Sure, Lacy. Glad to help."

Annie left the mayor's office thinking that her willing attitude had probably gotten her into her present trouble. But try as she might, she couldn't figure out a way to get out of the situation. Isabel and Carmen were waiting on Thomas and, as far as Annie could see, he was her only hope, too.

Briefly she considered going into Mexico to search for him. Lord! Wouldn't Brett have a fit if he knew that!

THE NEXT EVENING, she and Brett clashed, although not over the real issues.

"When you called, you said we had to talk. Here I am. And you're going out." Brett leaned against the door frame and watched Annie dress.

"I thought you'd be here earlier." She slipped into her slacks and pulled up the zipper.

"I was detained." He noted the gentle flare of her hips and felt the familiar craving to touch her.

She gave him an appealing look. "I wish you'd go with me tonight. The mayor requested that you be on this committee. Sure you won't change your mind?"

"I told you before, committee meetings don't appeal to me."

"Well, heck, I don't particularly like them, either. But there doesn't seem to be a better way to do a job democratically and efficiently."

"I'm tired tonight. I've been busy today."

"Me, too. So has everyone else on the committee."

"And I don't want to spend my evening listening to someone drone on about sewer systems or budgets."

"That isn't on our agenda tonight. We all have other jobs, Brett. Trouble is, if everyone had your attitude, nothing would get done. But the real clincher is that none of us will be able to survive here if Silverton dies. So somebody has to put in the night hours."

"I have other ideas for my night hours."

She bent over and tossed her hair to give it a fluffy appearance. From beneath the curtain of hair she mumbled, "Yeah. Play."

"So what's wrong with a little R and R? It's good for the soul. You ought to try it sometime, Annie, instead of indulging this workaholic attitude you have." He gestured with one hand and slapped his thigh in frustration.

She straightened and faced him. "Brett, we've all worked hard for the past couple of years for one thing— to save our little town. And that includes your father. With Lacy's guidance and everyone pulling together, we've improved the situation around here a lot. We have a few businesses and new ones on the horizon. We have new industries considering our town. Just look how the technical school has boosted our population and economy."

"I'll be the first to take my hat off to your successes," he agreed. "Hey, what everybody's done to salvage this place has been miraculous. But just make sure that you haven't forgotten how to play along the way." He took a seat on her bed and watched her pull on a striking jade-green sweater. The color matched her eyes, which tonight were flashing with the sparks he had ignited.

Annie tugged the tunic-length cotton knit over her hips. Her actions revealed the frustration that was building up inside her. Brett was definitely *not* going to be a part of this committee. And the responsibility of the refugees was a burden she couldn't share with him, either.

Gazing into the mirror, she saw a tight-lipped, sullen woman. She glanced over at Brett, lounging on her bed. Maybe he was right; she'd forgotten how to play.

"I have a farm that needs constant care, in case you haven't noticed by now," she said petulantly.

"Constant?" He shook his head. "Nothing's constant, Annie. What about a long weekend of three or four days? Wouldn't you love to get away from the pressures and the sameness for a little while?"

The tough facade she presented started to melt. "Yes, of course I would. I'm not made of stone."

"That's good."

Annie concentrated on her hair while Brett watched. Finally he switched the subject to something less heated and personal. "What committee did you say? Pioneers?"

"Yes. Our purpose is to create the Pioneer Museum."

"Is this the committee that Holt's involved with?"

She nodded and applied lipstick to a mouth that was too tight. He had a point. She hadn't stopped to relax in years. "Holt says the building will be finished in time for our fall fiesta, so we need to be working on content."

"Rusty plowshares and old quilts?"

"I suppose those would be included." She shrugged. "But we want ours to be more than that. We want to emphasize items that are particularly southwestern. For instance, one of the exhibits will be a folk arts display. That's what Lacy asked me to work on. She just mentioned that you might be interested."

"In folk art? Great. She wants me on a committee where I know absolutely nothing about the subject."

"Forget it, Brett. I'll tell her you aren't interested in anything but play."

"That's not true and you know it, Annie. Be fair."

"Well, I didn't know anything about folk art, either, until I heard about it. Here, it's stuff like this." Annie reached for a large straw bag and brought out a carefully wrapped item. "Here are some samples I'm taking along to show. These are Christmas tree ornaments that Diego gave my aunt and uncle over the years. Aren't they pretty? He made them from tin. It's practically a lost art."

Brett surveyed the shiny, intricately crafted article. "Tin art. The poor man's silver, they call it."

"Exactly," she said, encouraged by his response. "I'm sure there are many other things like this that are unique to our area. Like the clay dolls the Indians and early settlers used to make for their children. They made apple dolls, too."

"What's an apple doll?"

"You peel an apple and carve a face on one side. Then you set it in a dry place for several months. It turns into a wrinkled, funny face. And you have your apple doll. But I'm looking for beautiful and unique handcrafted items. Local weavers, for instance, raise the sheep, card and dye the wool, then weave it into beautiful blankets and rugs and other household items. I'm sure we'll feature some of their work."

He nodded thoughtfully. "My grandmother used to do some very nice embroidery work."

Annie paused and smiled at him. "That's what I'm talking about, Brett. We want crafts that were done so beautifully they can truly be called art. I'd love to see some of your grandmother's work. Do you have any of it?"

"I'll see if I can find anything packed away. J.M. kept everything."

"Great." She halted and looked at him. "You sure you don't want to go with me tonight?"

"You sure you don't want to stay home with me tonight?"

She felt the strong challenge to her willpower. Of course she'd rather be with him. She was only human. And he was...oh, so appealing, lounging on her bed, luring her with his dark, exotic eyes. "I'm tempted," she admitted. "In fact, I'd love to stay with you, Brett. But I promised to do my part for Silverton."

"I figure I'll do my part by working at the junior college."

She looked up quickly. "The junior college?"

"I have a part-time job teaching in the Criminal Justice Department." He shrugged. "That's why I was late coming over here tonight. I was conferring with the VP of Instruction and Curriculum on the courses I'll be teaching."

"Why, Brett, that's wonderful!" She gazed at him with open curiosity. "I didn't even know you were looking to teach. What course?"

"They're hiring me under a special program as a so-called expert in the field. So, because I'm not a traditionally trained teacher, I'll present specialized courses for the second-year students. One will be "Problems in Criminal Justice" and the other is a seminar on deviant behavior."

She stared at him. "D-deviant behavior?"

"Considering my years of experience dealing with various types of criminals, I should be able to handle that."

"Uh, yes. I'm sure."

"For the other course, I'll use actual case studies. Should be fun."

"You call that fun?" She blinked. Actual case studies? Perhaps hers?

He sat up and studied her bewildered expression. "Somehow I thought you'd be pleased, Annie."

"I am, yes, I really am. Just thrilled." She began searching for her running shoes in the bottom of the closet.

"I see. You just have a strange way of showing it."

"I'm in a hurry, that's all." As she fumbled with her shoes, her imagination whirled with images of Brett handcuffing her, pushing her past clicking cameras with her jacket draped over her head so no one would recognize her. She could hear him telling his father what she'd done, about her deviant behavior.

"Annie—"

"I'm pleased for you, Brett. What more do you expect me to say? I think this community is lucky to have you here to help solve the raging crime problems around our vicious neighborhoods."

"What's that supposed to mean?" He stood up and angrily took her in his arms. "What's wrong with you tonight, Annie?"

"Nothing."

"Not true. I can read you. Something's bothering you. What is it?"

"I told you. Nothing. I'm going to be late."

"Was it something I said. Or something I did?"

"No, of course not." She attempted to laugh, but the effort fell short.

He looked intently at her, searching her face for some clue. Her eyes were troubled and her mouth was pinched; the signs of anxiety were there. "Well, I can't make you tell me what you don't want me to know."

Feeling about as guilty as a person could, Annie placed her cheek against his in a brief hug. He was a rock, so straight-arrow and solid. How on earth could she tell him about her involvement with illegal refugees when she knew how terribly upset with her he would be. Why, he would probably—Her thoughts were brought up short when she realized she had no idea how he'd actually react. And there was only one way to find out.

"I have to go." She slipped from his embrace and grabbed her purse and the straw bag of tin ornaments.

Silently Brett followed her down the hall.

In the kitchen, she paused. "Brett...maybe when I get back, we'll discuss—" she took a breath "—a quick weekend somewhere."

"Can you spare the time?"

"This is what Aunt Annalee called 'the magic time' for apples. There isn't a lot of work to do while they're growing except watch for trouble and keep them watered. Diego can certainly do that for a couple of days."

"Okay." His reaction wasn't as jubilant as he had once thought it would be. It was such a quick shift for her that he was doubtful about her sincerity.

"We'll discuss it when I get back," she promised.

Brett walked her out to the Jeep. He caught her hand as she was about to open the door. "Do me a favor, Annie."

She gazed up at him, thinking that when those eyes settled on her, she would do anything he asked. She quickly kissed his lips. "What?"

He fumbled into his pocket and pulled out his keys. "Take my car tonight. It'll be much safer than that old Jeep of yours. Why, the thing might break down at any moment."

"Oh, no, I couldn't drive such a fancy car."

"It's a breeze. You don't know the dangerous elements that are out there. I do."

She sighed. "Well . . ."

"Anyway, I'm sure you'll enjoy the ride. It's much smoother than the Jeep. And all the doors will lock. Plus the engine is in tip-top shape—it won't stall."

"Are you through bashing my old reliable Jeep?"

"It's great for the rough stuff. But for you, I only want the best." With one arm tucked around her shoulders, he steered her toward the Mercedes.

Resigned to Brett's wish, Annie drove his car to the meeting. He was right. It was a much smoother ride. And she knew, as she gazed in awe at the lighted dashboard, that there was only one reason Brett insisted on doing this—he cared for her. She just hoped he cared enough to overlook her criminal behavior.

WHEN SHE RETURNED from her meeting, Brett was waiting. Annie knew that she should tell him what was going on, but they were supposed to discuss a possible trip.

She'd tell him later, when he would be in a better mood to understand....

She greeted him with a kiss. "Did you get some rest tonight?"

"Hmm. Who could rest while waiting on you?"

She pressed one finger to his chest. "You'd better, mister, after all the complaining and excuses I heard before this meeting."

"My heart pounded and my blood raced the whole time I was sitting here thinking about you." He began to kiss her earlobe and neck. "My palms got all sweaty. And my body heat increased twenty percent in anticipation of your return. Did you think of me this evening?"

"Only once. When Holt asked me if you were going to join the committee."

"And you said?"

"I said you probably would. Someday. If you didn't leave town first."

"I'm not leaving." He slipped his hands beneath her jacket to her waist. "What kind of a fool do you think I am?"

"Well, then, I guess you'll have to join sometime, won't you?"

He sighed and shook his head. "How can I tell you no?"

She smiled and turned around to kiss him. "You can't." She beckoned with one finger and a come-hither smile as she started toward the bedroom.

Brett followed her. "How did the meeting go?"

"Fine." She began undressing. "I have a lot to do before next meeting. And I'm going to need help."

"Don't tell me they elected you chairman!"

She waggled her hand. "No, that's Holt's job. But they loved the folk art idea. So we need to come up with as many examples as we can and decide on the display items."

"I'll help you."

She gazed at him curiously.

He ignored her and assisted in the matter of pulling off her clothes. "Hmm, you're lovely, Annie. So fair and delicate."

She grinned and nestled in the circle of his arms. "But we both know 'delicate' doesn't really describe me."

His lips teased her with tiny kisses. "Not by a long shot. Did we want to discuss San Francisco before or after?" His kisses grew longer and stronger.

When they paused for a breath, she murmured, "San Francisco's too far away. Takes too long to get there."

"We'd fly there in no time."

She shook her head. "Too expensive for me. We'd still have to drive to an airport in Albuquerque or Tucson."

"Annie, I'll pay. This will be my treat for us both."

"Oh, no. Not for me, you don't."

"Give me one sensible reason why I can't pay if I want to."

She kissed him. "Because..." she murmured against his lips. "I won't be a kept woman. But since I feel that we both need a little R and R, I'd be willing to consider going as far as Tucson. We could drive it almost as quickly as going to the Albuquerque airport."

He lifted his head and gazed at her, a million images dancing in his head. He didn't care where they went, really. He just wanted to whisk her away. "Why are you agreeing to do this, Annie?"

"Because of what you said about me working all the time. You're right. I haven't had a vacation in years. And I want you to see that I do know how to have fun." She wriggled her underwear-clad body against his. "Besides I want to be alone with you. With no interruptions."

"I concur completely." He spread his hands across her back. "Annie, all I want is to see you happy. And relaxed. And in my arms. And if you won't go to San Francisco, I'll settle for Tucson."

She smiled happily and abandoned herself to his arms and his kisses and his extremely pleasurable loving.

ON THURSDAY NIGHT, Annie decided to tell Carmen and Isabel of her plans to be gone for the weekend. It crossed her mind that Thomas might arrive, and they could be gone by the time she returned. Now, as she knocked on Diego's door, Annie had mixed emotions. She had wanted them to be gone for so long that it was strange to feel this sense of sadness.

Carmen opened the door slowly. Her expression was apprehensive, and she looked tired around the eyes. When she saw Annie, she smiled. "Hello, Annie."

"I just wanted to speak to you and Isabel for a minute. Hope I'm not too late."

"Isabel is asleep already," Carmen said in a hushed voice. "She was very tired tonight."

"Then, don't disturb her."

"Please come in. We can speak quietly." Carmen took a step backward and gestured for Annie to enter.

Carmen nervously fiddled with some needlework on which she'd apparently been working. "It is not...some bad news?"

"Not really—Oh, you mean bad news about Thomas? No, I haven't heard anything. Have you?"

"No. Nothing." Carmen shook her head.

Annie's gaze went to Carmen's nervous hands clutching the embroidered cloth, and spontaneously she reached out and patted them. "I'm sure he's okay, Carmen. Please, don't worry so much. It isn't good for your baby."

"I know. I try to be happy because you are so good to us. But, deep down, I am afraid for my Thomas. And for us all."

"I'm going to take care of you until he comes," Annie promised fervently. "And he will. Soon. I just know it."

"I pray you are right," Carmen said, rubbing her belly. "The baby, he is very active tonight."

Annie's smile brightened. "How do you know it's a boy?"

"He kicks like a soccer player, so strong." Carmen giggled and shifted. "Want to feel him?"

"Could I?" Annie scooted forward.

"*Sí.* Put your hand here." Carmen placed Annie's hand on one side of her protruding belly and shifted her position again.

In a few seconds, Annie felt the gentle thump-thump of the baby's movement against Carmen's body. "Oh! There it is!" She clamped her other hand over her mouth to muffle the squeals of excitement that bubbled from her throat.

Carmen smiled proudly. "He's strong enough to be a boy, *sí*?"

"Yeah, I agree. Oh, that must be thrilling."

Carmen nodded. "I want to share this joy with *mi* Thomas, but at least Isabel is here with me. And you and Diego."

Annie realized that in a strange way, she and Diego had become a surrogate family for this young woman who was so far from her real family. It made thoughts of her leaving even harder.

"I know it's rough without him," Annie said, "but you mustn't lose faith." She leaned forward with elbows on her knees. "I have to tell you that I'm taking a short trip this weekend, Carmen. I'll only be gone a few days to Tucson. I'll be back Sunday evening."

"Oh, no, do not leave us! What if . . . what if Thomas comes?"

"That's why I'm telling you. I want you to go on and do whatever is best. If you must be on your way, then I will understand. You must not wait for me."

"My good friend, Annie. We might not see you again."

Annie nodded solemnly. "I want you to know that I care very much what happens to you. I hope you will all be safe in your journey. If you ever need any help in your new life, please let me know, and I'll do what I can. And when you reach your new home, please write me. Here is my address." She gave Carmen a slip of paper. "I want to know where you are and how you're doing. And all about the baby."

Carmen rose and wrapped her slender arms around Annie, hugging her tight. Annie returned the gesture and, in the closeness, felt the baby kicking Carmen's belly again.

As she walked away from the shed, Annie wiped a tear. She had never felt so emotionally torn. When she was with Brett, she knew the gravity of her crime. And, mentally, she agreed it was wrong.

But when she was with Carmen, she didn't care about laws. She cared only about these people. And making sure they were safe was the right—and only—thing to do.

9

IT WAS JUNE in Tucson. And it was hot.

"Only one solution…" Brett murmured as he lounged lazily on the giant bed and patted the empty space next to him.

"Only one?" Annie cast him a teasing glance, then proceeded to explore their resort-style surroundings with a youthful delight. "I'll bet I could come up with a dozen ideas for keeping cool. Just look at this place! Oh, Brett, La Paloma is beautiful! I'm so glad you picked this spot! The room is perfect! The view is magnificent!" She stood before the sliding glass doors that opened onto a small balcony, and took a deep, satisfying breath. Then, she beckoned to him with one finger. "It's the perfect place for us."

"I only know of one perfection," he murmured in a low voice. "One particularly perfect lady. She's absolutely breathtaking." With a grin he left the bed and joined her, curling his arm around her shoulders. "Takes my breath, anyway."

"The view does that to you."

"*You* do that to me." He squeezed her shoulders as they both took in the magnificent scene before them.

The Catalina Mountains created a northern border for Tucson and the La Paloma Resort, where a verdant golf course rambled outside desert-pink buildings. An inner courtyard presented desert gardens interspersed with a waterfall, the pool and various patios for the guests' eating and relaxation.

"Nice," he said mildly.

"Nice? It's fabulous! That pool looks so inviting!"

The pool flowed beneath a small arched bridge that separated the deep end, and a water-level bar, from the shallow children's section.

"Want to try it?" he asked, admitting that it was, indeed, inviting. The drive from Silverton to Tucson had been warm, in spite of the air-conditioned car.

"Yes!" She started unbuttoning her blouse. "How did you ever guess?"

Her enthusiasm was contagious, and Brett whirled her into his arms and around the room, kissing her lips and neck and, finally, her half-exposed breasts.

Laughing with joy, she clung to his neck, and when he stopped kissing her, she spontaneously reached up and kissed him again. "Brett, I love being with you . . . love every moment we're together."

He gazed at her with a warmth he hadn't experienced in years. "Surely you know I feel the same way, Annie. You're beauty and joy. You give me a renewed enthusiasm for life that I'll admit I'd lost before I came back to Silverton. You've shown me beauty where I'd forgotten there was any."

"I'm glad—" she paused shyly "—to know you feel that way about Silverton. I thought, for a while, that you hated it."

He shook his head. "I hated everything else about my life. Now I see that Silverton—and especially you—are the best things that have happened to me in a long, long time."

Annie felt ebullience and hope spreading like warm honey through her body. Maybe she wasn't throwing away her love, after all. "This was a great idea, to get away, alone, and explore our feelings. And share our love."

He nuzzled her neck. "I *know* how I feel when I'm around you, Annie. I want to love you all the time."

"I feel the same way, Brett." She giggled as his hot breath tickled her, then her voice grew low and serious. "But I want to know if this rush is more than lust."

"What's wrong with a little lust?"

"Nothing. We can explore that, too . . . after a swim." She twirled away from his arms and grabbed a polka-dot swimsuit from her suitcase. Dangling the tiny item at arm's length, she wriggled her eyebrows tauntingly. "Wouldn't you like to see this on?"

"I'd rather see the exciting parts that fit into it." He made a lunge toward her.

She laughed and dashed into the bathroom, just barely out of his reach.

THEY PLAYED in the pool for a while, and when they returned to the room, a bottle of chilled champagne awaited them.

Brett assumed the job of popping the cork.

Annie sat at the bottom of the bed and watched as he grasped the bottle and twisted off the wire holding the cap. With a little finesse and flair, he eased the cork out of the bottle with a muffled pop! His hands dwarfed the crystal goblets as he poured them each a glass of wine, then returned the bottle to the ice bucket.

With a flourish he presented her with a goblet, then sat beside her and insisted that they link arms to drink. Before the act was completed, each had laughingly spilled chilled champagne on the other, and attempts to lap up the mess led to succulent kisses. . . .

Annie turned her face up to receive his thirsty kisses. And then, with an appetite of her own, she returned his ravenous affection. She felt his tongue slide along the line of her lips and opened immediately to the gentle probing. He tasted of mint and champagne and the nebulous essence of growing desire. As his kisses intensified and her responses blossomed, Annie felt an exciting and wonderful passion bubbling through her like champagne.

Brett paused long enough to take another sip from his goblet and encouraged her to do the same. Then he set their glasses aside.

Dazed by the combination of champagne and intoxicating sensuality, Annie remained seated while Brett placed one bent knee beside her and leaned to kiss her earlobe, then her neck. Sweet kisses followed his hands along each shoulder as he slid the straps of her bikini top down. Annie gasped softly, her body responding with a pulsating warmth to each moist kiss. His hands framed her bare ribs, then moved up to the sides of her breasts, caressing the sensitive skin. He reached around her back, where he swiftly unlatched the binding swimsuit top and removed it.

Her bare breasts were achingly full and seemed to fit naturally into the cupped palms of his hands. He lifted and admired and gently buffed both at the same time with a sureness of knowing her reactions. He squeezed the magenta tips between his thumbs and forefingers until she moaned with the tormenting pleasure.

She reached out, wanting to draw him to her, and met the muscular power of his naked thigh. She felt the warm flesh beneath her fingers and slid her exploring hand up his thigh until she found his maleness.

"Annie..." He muttered roughly and pulled her to her feet. Wedging her firmly between his thighs, he quickly skimmed the bottom of her swimsuit off. As he stroked her naked hips, he thrust his engorged fullness against her belly.

With a boldness that surprised her, Annie stripped off his swimsuit, too, and for a heated moment, they stood mere inches apart, naked and wanting, caressing lightly, their brief resistance only increasing the fires that flamed their passion. His body expanded toward her, as if reaching out to include her, and she delighted in the brown smoothness of him, the extreme masculinity he exuded.

He took one of her hands and pressed the palm to his lips, kissing and laving the center with his tongue. The action sent spirals of desire shooting through her, and she thought she'd crumble if he didn't take her soon.

"Brett . . . please . . ." She ended with a gasp and quick intake of breath.

"Patience, my love. Seeing you like this," he whispered hoarsely, "drives me crazy, I want you so badly." He slipped his hand between her legs, caressing the sweet tenderness he found there. "Now, Annie. You want me, too."

She nodded, knowing she couldn't bear much more of this physical torment. Stepping forward, she taunted him by brushing her silky femininity against his taut body. Throwing her head back, she closed her eyes, relishing the tantalizing sensations his hard-muscled body created within her. She lifted her arms above her head, arching her back, and swayed, each movement causing additional friction of body against body, heat magnifying heat. With the gracefulness of a dancer, she lowered her hands to his shoulders, skimming along the surface of his skin, enjoying the torrid reactions she could see, *feel*, as he tried to resist her.

He mumbled something practically unintelligible, and she understood only "Now!" as he moved, stumbling backward in his haste, to his suitcase. "As soon as I take care of this protection business." In a brief minute, he returned and slumped into the boudoir chair. "Come here, Annie," he murmured in a low, sexy voice.

With a slow smile, she walked toward him. Desire built inside her with each step until she was like a coiled spring standing before his wide-spread knees. Placing her hands on his shoulders, she straddled his lap, facing him. Her lips tightened into a determined line as she maneuvered her body over his. Then, slowly, ever so slowly, she lowered herself over him until they merged.

He leaned forward, kissing her lips with a feverish strength, forcing them apart for the entry of his tongue. She felt his manhood filling her up, even as his tongue sought the honeyed recesses of her mouth. The dual sensations seemed to ignite her entire being, casting her into an erotic frenzy. She arched and felt him swelling even further.

They were together now, as they were meant to be, fully and completely. Oh, how she wanted him—wanted him forever. Every part of her ached for him, and she began to move beyond her awareness, rhythmically rocking, reaching the bounds of sensuous pleasure and plunging beyond. Barely cognizant of her actions, only of the man in her control, Annie ascended to the brink of ecstasy, then rose to a high, envious, climactic peak.

While she was still reeling, she felt Brett's powerful explosion.

Repeated volleys of desire rolled through her, rising in her with fierce intensity, crashing in a flood of relief, then building again. For a while she thought the frenzy would never end. She wished it wouldn't as she clung to his shoulders and cried his name.

Finally she sank onto him, sated and fulfilled as she had never been before. The two clung together, hands clutching, perspiration mingling. Completely and totally enmeshed. Content with each other. Needing no one else. Annie drifted somewhere between heaven and the most wonderful earth she had ever experienced.

Brett stroked her back, feeling toward this woman as he had never felt toward any other. He was a dominating man, in control of himself and his destiny, and he liked to dominate his women.

Now, here was this small dynamo with wild strawberry-blond hair and devilish green eyes who had captured him completely. *She* dominated him, body and soul, spirit and emotion, without lifting a finger. Without an element of aggression, she could have her way with him, and strangely he would go willingly.

She stirred, lifting her head. Moist curls straggled around her face. His chest glistened with a healthy sheen. They had shared everything—their lives, their bodies, their love . . . everything but an avowal of that love. Oh, how Annie wondered about that.

"We have something special, you know," she began hesitantly.

"Yeah." Eyes still heavy with passion, he nodded. "I'm not sure I understand it yet. But I'm working on it."

She lowered herself to his chest again, pressing her breasts to him, her cheek to his smooth skin. Perhaps she shouldn't say it. Or perhaps she didn't trust looking at him when she confessed. "I'm afraid . . . I love you, Brett."

He sighed. "I'm afraid so, too." He knew he should be saying "Me, too," but he wasn't. Couldn't.

Annie shivered. It wasn't the answer she wanted. *Needed.* "Brett . . ." She would tell him that he didn't have to concur, that she wouldn't create a problem over this.

But he stopped her. His voice was quiet. "We're like two magnets. Drawn together in spite of . . . everything."

"In spite of not wanting."

"Maybe. I'll admit I didn't come to Silverton to fall in love."

"Or to settle down."

"Yeah." He almost growled the word.

"I hope I haven't caused you trouble, Brett."

"Of course not. You're no trouble. You're . . . the only light in my life, Annie."

She caught her breath. What was he saying? Maybe the more important thing was what he *wasn't* saying. "I didn't mean to embarrass you, Brett. Or put you on the spot. But I don't take this kind of relationship with a man lightly. And I wanted you to know that my feelings are running deep. Maybe too deep."

"I . . . don't want to hurt you, Annie."

"There's only one way you could do that, Brett." She knew that if he ever left, she would crumble inside. He knew it, too.

"Only one?" he repeated with a sad chuckle. "I'm sure I could think of a dozen. And I don't want to. Believe me, Annie."

After a moment of strained silence, she said, "I believe you, Brett."

The wild lovemaking had added another dimension to their relationship. But the little conversation afterward had left them pensive and withdrawn to inner thoughts they were reluctant to share right now.

Rather than eat in the hotel's fancy restaurants that night, they chose to seek a Mexican restaurant downtown. Taking the recommendation of one of the hotel busboys, they crossed the bridge over the mostly dry riverbed of the Rillito River and discovered the authentic Casa Molina, an establishment run for generations by a local family.

Replenished by the Mexican music and food, Brett reminisced about his childhood. "Family was very important to us, especially to my mother. All her relatives would gather, usually at our house, and eat and sing some of the old songs from Mexico. Those songs sounded very foreign to me, but now when I hear them, they're familiar."

"Do you know the words?"

"Not all of them. But the words aren't really that important. It's the emotion that's felt in the songs. And that's apparent whether you understand or not."

"You're right," she agreed. "I love some of the songs, but have no idea what they're saying."

"I particularly remember my grandfather and his brother. *Los abuelos*, the grandfathers, we called them. They would sing together and, even at their advanced ages, they could harmonize beautifully. Their favorite was an old song called 'Volver, Volver.'"

"Return, return?"

"They used to sing of returning to Mexico. Actually, many of the old ones were born in Mexico, but when Arizona and New Mexico made statehood in 1912, what was once their Mexican homeland became the United States. As you might imagine, they greeted that with mixed emotions."

"It sounds like you have some wonderful childhood memories, Brett."

He reflected for a moment. "Some of them were. Not all, though."

The waiter appeared with their bill, and Annie decided not to pursue the matter now. On the way out of the restaurant, she spotted a small poster advertising a mariachi *espectacular* tomorrow in the downtown plaza.

"We could go, Brett. Oh, please. I'd love it. You would, too." She squeezed his hand. "You know you would." She could see the reluctance in his eyes, but she couldn't understand why. "Come on, Brett! This is a rare opportunity for me."

"For me, too." He gazed down at her, his dark expression softening. "All right. *Para ti*," he agreed in Spanish. *For you.* See what control she had over him?

THE NEXT DAY, the Mexican festivities in the plaza proved to be nostalgic for Brett. He explained the traditions that Annie didn't understand and, in the process, examined them in his own mind. Soon they found themselves caught up in the gaiety of the day, and whatever strain had existed between them vanished.

They mingled among the street vendors, eating hot tamales cooked the old-fashioned way in corn husks and nibbling fruit ice to keep cool. She bought him a straw sombrero with a bright red hatband. He bought her a lovely shawl with intricate embroidery around the edges that evolved into long, decorative fringe.

Various mariachi groups performed traditional music, and dancers in brightly colored costumes entertained the crowd. Annie glanced at Brett. He had been so reluctant to come today, she'd wondered if he would enjoy it. But the rapt expression on his face revealed more happiness than she had ever seen. And it made her feel good that she had insisted on the expedition.

In a special appearance, the famous pop singer from Tucson, Linda Ronstadt, joined her father and sister for a couple of songs. One was obviously a crowd favorite, "Volver, Volver."

Annie leaned close to Brett's ear as the family on stage blended their harmonic voices. "Is that the song you told me about? The one your grandfathers sang?"

Brett nodded. He seemed to be mesmerized or perhaps transported to another time and place. Annie didn't interrupt his reverie, but just held his hand.

The grand finale, held against the backdrop of a spectacular sunset of golds and oranges and brilliant pinks, presented a rousing song featuring all the day's performers. Young dancers, swishing their full colorful skirts, surrounded the stage and mingled with the crowd. The stage was filled with the mariachi groups as well as small children with their violins and guitars and trumpets, all wearing costumes, becoming a part of the traditions. They were the future, the keepers of the flame.

When it was over and the crowd started milling around in the twilight, Annie said sincerely, "This was the most spectacular event I've ever attended. I'm so glad we came."

"Me, too." Brett's voice was low and strangely quiet.

Annie smiled happily, knowing they had shared something else very special, and it could only bring them closer. "The Mexican culture is expressed so beautifully through their music. And I'm glad to see that they're keeping it alive with the children."

"Some things," he responded solemnly, "are worth saving."

"Yes. And these traditions definitely are." Annie clung to his arm as they maneuvered through the crowd. She wondered privately what Brett considered worth saving. Cultural traditions? An old family ranch that never reached expectations? Their relationship? She supposed time would tell about all those things. No one, not even Brett, knew the answers tonight.

ALL TOO SOON, their long "escape" weekend was over, and they headed back to Silverton. The bonds they had forged were difficult to assess at the time, but Annie found herself wondering how she had managed before Brett entered her life. She knew that before, she'd merely been existing, proceeding with the necessary acts to keep the apple farm going and profitable. Her social life had dwindled to practically nothing, and she had been totally lacking in the kind of emotional relationship she needed.

Annie felt that in spite of their differences, she had that kind of special relationship with Brett. She could only hope it would last. But that would depend on him.

As soon as they pulled into the driveway, Annie was thrust back into her highly charged and dangerous position with the refugees hiding on her farm. When she got out of the car, she looked around anxiously. No one was in sight, but she could *feel* eyes peering at them through the darkness. Brett took the heavy suitcase ahead, and she followed with a shopping bag of gifts they had purchased.

A willowy woman with long, dark hair and a big belly stepped from the darkness and hugged Annie. "Señorita Annie, I am so glad you are back."

"Carmen, you're still here." Annie couldn't help feeling a little relief. She would have hated for them to be gone before she returned, though she didn't know why. "How are you and the baby? And Isabel?"

"Fine. All are fine."

"Have you heard from Thomas?"

"No! Nothing! I am worried sick about him. I am afraid something bad has happened to him. What if—"

Annie interrupted. "Everything is going to be all right, Carmen. Don't lose hope. We . . . I'll try to find out next week where he might be."

"Oh, *señorita!* Would you?"

"I'll try. I'm not sure how, but I'll see if anyone knows anything about him."

Carmen hugged her again. "Oh, thank you! You are a good friend, Annie!"

"I've got to go now," Annie whispered. "I'll talk to you later. After he leaves." She nodded in the direction Brett had taken. She looked up and saw that Brett stood waiting for her on the porch steps. He had witnessed the emotional exchange with Carmen. Annie hurried toward him.

"She's living here?" he observed coolly.

Annie fiddled with the locked door and led the way inside. "Yes, she is. For a little while."

"Is she working for you?"

"Uh, yes." Annie switched the light on and dumped her parcels into the first chair. "This has been a great weekend, Brett. I'm so glad we went. I needed it. And I think you did, too."

He nodded. "I enjoyed it very much. You know that." He placed the suitcase in the hall and turned back to her, a puzzled expression on his face. "She isn't the woman I saw here the other morning."

"No, that was, uh, her mother-in-law."

"Oh. So she's one of the migrants who's helped you with the blossom thinning?"

Annie nodded. Why was he questioning her like this? Why was she holding back? They had shared so much this weekend, there should be no secrets between them. Maybe it was time to tell him.

"That woman looked pregnant, Annie."

"She is."

"Is it safe for you to hire a pregnant migrant worker? What if she has the baby here? What if—"

"Brett, please." Annie raised one hand to stop his questions. "This is probably a good time to tell you something I've been intending to for a long time."

He stuffed his hands into his jeans pockets and gave her his silent attention.

"They, uh, Isabel and Carmen aren't *exactly* migrants."

His face was dark, and she wondered what he was thinking. And if he knew.

"Then what . . . *exactly*, are they?"

"Brett, I want you to try to understand my position here. I didn't intend for this to happen. And I didn't purposely keep secrets from you. . . ." She paused. "Well, yes, to be perfectly honest, I guess I kept this one until . . . I knew I could trust you." She rushed on. "But it got worse when you took the special assignment with your dad. And worse yet when you agreed to teach criminal justice."

He gazed steadily at her. She was hiding something from him. And she did it poorly. Maybe it was a good sign that she couldn't lie readily. But deep in his heart, he suspected—and feared—what she would say next. And he feared his own reaction.

"Brett, I . . . I'm—" After a couple of ragged false starts, she took a deep breath and proceeded quickly. "I'm harboring refugees from Nicaragua. They hid on my farm, waiting on an additional member of their party who's been delayed somewhere along the way, probably in Mexico. Their connection was broken and never completed. Then these women got sick. They needed help. And I agreed to see what I could do. I didn't expect them to stay this long, but...." She ended with a helpless shrug.

Brett listened to her rapid-fire spiel in stone silence. His dark eyes were expressionless. His chin became set. It had been a rambling rush of words, intended to manipulate his feelings by invoking his trust and understanding. He had heard such confessions before. And he understood that. When she finally hushed, he asked, "Why now, Annie? Why are you telling me this now? Why not earlier? Why tell me at all?"

"You're angry."

"No. I just want some answers."

"I really don't like the idea of keeping secrets from you, Brett. That isn't my way. Surely you know that by now. I want you to know what I'm doing. And why. I want you to understand."

"What I can understand is your agitation at finding illegals on your property. And what I can do about that is to make a single phone call and have them picked up. I can get them out of your hair."

She hadn't expected this reaction at all. She seized his arm with a frantic grip. "No, you can't do that, Brett!"

"I will see that you aren't involved. We'll just take them—"

"No! Brett, you mustn't do that!" Panic flooded through her and hot tears stung her eyes. She hadn't expected such a coldhearted solution from Brett, the man she loved. She expected him to understand. "These women are refugees. They'll be killed if you send them back."

"Sounds like they've convinced you of that."

"I believe them, Brett." Her heart pounded solidly inside her breast. "I'm already involved with these people. I've taken them to the doctor. Dr. Theresa knows about them."

"But when you became involved, you didn't know their status?"

She nodded slowly, reluctantly admitting full guilt. "Yes, I did. And I've continued to harbor them for their safety."

His eyes shot dark daggers as his anger exploded. "Annie, that was really stupid of you to get involved!"

"Isabel was quite sick from undiagnosed diabetes. She was a woman in great need, and I couldn't turn my back on her." Annie squared her shoulders proudly. There was no regret in her words. "I gave her safe harbor. And Diego gave up his room for them."

"So the two of you have collaborated on this?"

"If you want to put it that way, yes. We kept the secret between us."

"So you have two Nicaraguan women here. One has diabetes. The other one is . . . pregnant."

Annie nodded.

Brett shook his head in dismay. "Annie, you are in deep trouble. They have to go!"

"And they will, too. As soon as Carmen's husband gets here."

"Now!"

"No! They have nowhere to go. They have no one. No one but me."

"So you're admitting that you're giving illegals sanctuary. You refuse to turn them in. You refuse to let me pick them up and send them back home where they belong."

"Yes."

"Why, Annie? Don't you know the gravity of your situation?"

"Sort of." She twisted her hands. "But I can't help it. I'm all they have. They trust me. And I won't break that trust."

"I trusted you, too, Annie."

"I know. That's why I couldn't continue this lie." She sighed and looked away from his steely gaze. "I guess I'm not as sweet and innocent as you think."

"I guess not! I almost wish you'd continued to lie. I liked you better that way."

"I'm sorry, Brett. I'd hoped you'd understand the truth."

"Do you fully appreciate my position here?"

"I know I've put you in a bad position."

"Bad? It's hellish!" He stormed toward the door.

She followed. "Brett, what are you going to do?"

"I didn't promise anything, Annie. To you or to your illegal aliens."

"Don't do anything, Brett! Please, just stay out of it!"

"How can I?"

She tried to cling to his arm, but he broke free and left her alone. Alone . . . except for her refugees. Her innocent victims. Her wards. Even if Brett turned his back on her, she couldn't abandon them now. A little voice deep inside her insisted that she was right.

And another voice said she was a fool.

10

ANNIE SHIVERED and pulled the new shawl Brett had bought her in Tucson tighter around her shoulders. She had spent a miserable, sleepless night after Brett left so abruptly. Dawn found her at the special place where she worked out so many of her problems.

"What am I going to do now, Aunt Annalee?" she murmured half aloud.

She made her way through the weeds to the mission ruins. The new-morning light reflected pale pink on the old bricks, giving it an eerie glow.

"I've ruined everything," she continued. "I thought I was doing the right thing by telling Brett about my refugees. But he was so furious last night, there's no way of knowing exactly what he'll do. He's law and order, through and through. He'll probably report them today, if he hasn't already. Report me, too."

She walked around one of the crumbling walls to the place where she first found the refugees hiding. "And I'm sure that all this will put an end to our relationship. He's too rigid in his beliefs." She kicked at a clump of grass. "And so am I."

Annie waited, listening, watching, hoping for a sign. Silence.

Frustrated, Annie lashed out at the invisible spirits of the mission. "Didn't you tell me to help them in the beginning? Well, I did. And now look where it got me. In big trouble! You know, I could be arrested for this!" She paused and chuckled bitterly. "In fact, Brett could arrest me. Wouldn't that be a nice twist."

She walked through the empty center of the old mission. It wasn't hard to imagine rows of benches where people sat to worship. And the section that would have been the church altar. A circle of bricks revealed a blackened area and small bits of charcoaled wood, proof of a recent fire. People were still using this old mission as a *santuario*.

She remembered once when a prison escapee had hidden out in a nearby church. He held officers at bay for three days until he finally decided to give up. The minute he emerged from the building, the arms of the law surrounded him. When she asked why the sheriff didn't just go in after him, Aunt Annalee had explained that a church, or any holy place, traditionally constituted a sanctuary or asylum and immunity from arrest.

Which is exactly what Isabel and Carmen had done.

And since the *santuario* was on Annie's property, what was so wrong about her allowing their immunity?

With renewed spirits and a determined gleam in her eyes, Annie walked back to her Jeep and headed directly for Brett's house.

He was mulling over a cup of coffee when he heard her Jeep. He wasn't surprised to see her at this hour; he had known she wouldn't give up her principles without a fight. Not Annie. But then, neither would he.

Annie mustered her courage and knocked, knowing that anything and everything she said could be used against her in a court of law. That was a terrible thing to consider about the man she loved.

Brett opened the door, looking about as disheveled as she had ever seen him. Darkly devastating eyes, red rimmed. Usually neat black hair, a mess. Square, ordinarily clean-shaven chin, darkly shadowed with bristle. At first she thought she had awakened him. Then she smelled coffee and realized that he was probably as agitated as she over this—and had probably spent as restless a night.

That, she decided, was some consolation. Maybe, just maybe, he hadn't reported her to the authorities yet. And she still had a chance to plead her case.

As she stood for a brief but seemingly endless moment, silently gazing at this man who could destroy her, Annie was stricken with the singular thought that he was truly wonderful and that, amazingly, she loved him. *Still.* She wondered—crazily—if she would love him *still* if he arrested her. A part of her wanted to reach out and take his hands, to kiss his lips, to feel his strong, comforting arms around her. But that was nonsense. She was letting emotions squeeze into a grave situation where they had no place.

"Annie—" Brett took a ragged breath at the compelling sight of her dressed in jeans and clutching that beautiful shawl he had bought her just two days ago. He remembered making love to her, wrapping her naked body in that very shawl. Oh, how he ached to hold her again, to spread his fingers through her hair, as he had done last weekend. He yearned to crush her to him and protect her from this bizarre situation, to assure her that everything would be all right. But he couldn't. He was too damn stubborn. "Come in. Coffee?" He sounded strangely as if nothing unusual had happened.

"Yes, thanks." She sat at the table, squeezing her hands together, waiting for him to pour and serve the coffee.

"Don't tell me you were just in the neighborhood at—" he glanced at the stove clock "—seven-o-three in the morning."

"Something like that." She hooked her hands around the steaming cup he placed before her and waited until he took a chair. "Actually, I made a special trip over here to ask you—to beg, if necessary—to leave my refugees alone. They'll be gone soon, out of your life and mine. I promise."

He pressed his lips together grimly. She obviously hadn't budged in her opinion. "*Your* refugees?"

"I guess at this point I feel a little possessive. Their problems have become my problems."

"Only because you've made them yours."

"I couldn't turn these people away. Right or wrong, I just couldn't, Brett."

"And you're asking me to look the other way, too."

She nodded. "Is it too much to ask? We're more than neighbors, aren't we? More than friends?"

He licked his lips and turned his head, avoiding those dagger-sharp green eyes of hers. Why couldn't he just take charge here, the way he'd always been able to do before? Just tell her! Right is right and wrong is . . . not okay, even for her, especially for him.

"Yes, of course we're more than . . ." He paused to take a deep breath. "We're lovers, for Pete's sake! We're close, damn close. I care for you, Annie, about what happens to you."

"Then why can't you do as I ask, just this once?"

"Come on, Annie. How would it look for a college professor teaching ethics and criminology, someone who's ex-FBI and now a special agent for the sheriff's department to be aware of illegals living here?"

"But they're refugees, not illegals! There's a difference!"

"Not in the eyes of the law. Nor to me. Annie, I could lose my jobs. This constitutes accomplice."

"No one will ever know."

"Aggh!"

"Don't you believe in the old custom of sanctuary, Brett? It's long been traditional in these parts that people are safe in a church."

"That's ridiculous."

"Are you saying that some traditions aren't worth saving?"

"Maybe."

"So, in your selective opinion, certain songs and dances are worth saving as entertainment, but traditions that assist people should be discarded."

"Annie—" He halted, frustrated with the futility of this argument. She was so damned distracting, he just wanted to grab her up in his arms. Softening his voice, he persisted. "Annie, dear, your back shed is no church."

"No, but the mission ruin is. And that's where they first sought sanctuary. In fact, their plan was to move on swiftly, not to stay. But they ran into problems beyond their control."

"Legally, they cannot stay. And you are subject to federal prosecution by harboring them."

"I know a little about laws, too, Brett," she countered. "According to the 1980 Refugee Act, people who are in fear of their lives can seek asylum in this country."

"The question then becomes whether they are in fear of their lives."

"They say they are. And I believe them." Her green eyes narrowed in her intense fervor. "The problem seems to be coming from our government's perception that these people's lives are not in danger. While their perception is that they're fleeing for their lives."

"You may have a point, Annie. But are you prepared to take on the federal government?"

"No. I hope it won't come to that. Please, Brett, before you close your mind completely, come with me to meet them."

"Meet them? What makes you think I have any desire to meet them?"

She reached across the table and squeezed his hand. "I know you aren't so cold that you don't think of the people affected by the laws."

He scoffed and glanced down at her slender hand, pale against his, looking much weaker and smaller. Yet, with her powerful energy and control, she could rule him. Maybe . . . maybe she had a point worth reviewing.

She could see his hesitation and hurried on with her reasoning. "Isabel and Carmen are real people. They're ordinary, average women, good people. When you meet them, you'll see why I care about them." She leaned forward earnestly and surrounded his hand with both of hers. "Oh, Brett, I'm talking about somebody's mother and someone's wife who's going to have a baby soon.

And she doesn't know where her husband is—or even if he's alive. Can't you sympathize with them?"

"Annie, you are such a softhearted person. And to show you that my heart isn't made entirely of stone, the way you seem to think it is, I'll go meet them."

Instantly she was on her feet, rushing forward to embrace him. "I knew you would," she murmured against his chest. "I knew you would!"

"I haven't agreed to anything, Annie. Just to meet them."

"I know." She smiled up at him. "That's enough."

He cupped her face with both hands. "You are quite persuasive."

"I hoped you couldn't refuse me, Brett."

"That's my biggest problem, Annie. I can't refuse you." His claim melted into a kiss that extended into a five-minute blending of lips and tongues and hearts.

When he finally tore himself away from her and went to get his boots, Brett chastised himself for allowing her hope. He knew her scheme. She was using her feminine power over his weakness for her. Annie was banking on the possibility that he couldn't look these women in the eye and send them back where they came from. Well, she was wrong. He had worked undercover. He had made friends with the worst and the best—and turned around and arrested them when the line of the law was crossed.

BY THE TIME they arrived at Annie's shed, Isabel and Carmen were returning from breakfast in the big house. Diego was with them, as he sometimes joined them for the early meal. When he saw Annie lead Brett into the shed, he dropped back and headed for the nearest orchard.

"Isabel, this is my friend, Brett Meyer," Annie said, pulling Brett forward. "Brett, this is Isabel."

Brett took her hand. "*Mi gusto*, my pleasure."

Isabel hid an embarrassed grin behind her hand, for it was obvious that she recognized him as the man she had caught nude in Annie's kitchen.

"And this is Carmen." Annie put an arm around Carmen's shoulders. "This is my friend, Brett Meyer."

Carmen stiffened when she saw him and heard his name. Her dark eyes shifted quickly to Annie. "Is he the one who is worse than the border patrol?"

Brett cleared his throat and glared at Annie.

"No, Carmen," Annie assured her. "No worse. Brett is my friend. And he may be able to help us."

Carmen's demeanor changed visibly. She smiled hopefully at Brett. "Yes? You could help? Maybe you can find my Thomas. We believe he is somewhere in Mexico."

"I don't know about that." He cast a furious glance at Annie and pulled her aside. "I did *not* say I would help do anything like this," he muttered in a whisper.

She patted his hand. "I know. But Thomas is missing. And look at poor Carmen. She's desperate, and so am I. If anyone could find him, you could, Brett."

"Wrong, Annie! I have no intention of searching for an illegal Nicaraguan in Mexico!"

Annie quieted him with a frown and a little shh-shh. "We'll talk about this later. Right now, I'd like you to get to know Isabel and Carmen." She pulled him back to the women. "Please, *señores*, tell my friend a little about your life back home. And what circumstances made you come here."

Isabel sat in a small rocker in the corner and nervously picked up her embroidery handwork. "We had homes. And a big *rancho*. They killed my husband and took over our business. We had to run for our lives." She began to rock furiously.

Annie sat beside Isabel on a little stool and patted her hands. "We're sorry to hear about your husband, Isabel."

"They would have killed my Thomas, too," Carmen added angrily, "if he did not hide like a criminal. That is how we became separated. We ran like chickens. And Thomas . . ." She shook her head. "He had to stay hidden. But someone was to bring him here. We pay *mucho dinero*, but he is not here yet. And we do not know where he is." She gestured skyward, then sat heavily in another chair, cupping her hands protectively around her swollen belly.

"What kind of business did you have?" Brett asked.

"We grow many fruits for the market and *mucho* coffee," Isabel answered. "But they took it all."

"They even took my school," Carmen said. "I taught children to dance. We had a wonderful time. But after the shootings, no one would send their children to my school anymore. I cannot blame them." She shook her head sadly. "And now we have nothing. Not Papa Julio. Not even my Thomas. *¿Quién sabe dónde es?*"

Annie gave Brett a defiant expression. "See? They fled for their lives. And now they need help. How could I refuse?" Her look also asked how he could refuse.

Brett spread his hands and shrugged. "Sounds like you folks could be entitled to admittance into this country as refugees. Some legal methods need to be followed. I'll uh . . ." He sighed and glanced at Annie. "I'll see what I can do."

"And see about Thomas, too?" Annie asked quickly.

He nodded. "I'll try. No promises, though." He glanced down at the work in Isabel's lap. "That's very beautiful. It looks like some of the embroidery my grandmother used to do. I've never seen any like it since."

"Is very old style," Isabel said. "Colcha, it is called."

Brett leaned close and examined the piece. "*Mi abuelita* did this colcha embroidery. The Spanish settlers brought it to this country many years ago."

Both Isabel and Carmen responded warmly when Brett used the Spanish word for *grandmother*. As he talked with them about their homeland and questioned them about Thomas's circumstances and what the future might hold, they gradually lost their wariness of him. Annie was impressed with his appearance of genuine concern. She hoped he was as sincere as he sounded and that he would be able to help find Thomas.

When they left the little room in the shed, Brett and Annie didn't notice that someone was watching from behind the truck.

They walked quietly into the kitchen to discuss their next strategy. Annie wondered what was going through his mind, if he was sincere, if he could actually help them become legal refugees. If he *would* help them.

"Well, Brett, what do you think? Am I still subject to house arrest?"

He chuckled. "Not by me. Actually, it looks pretty good for you. And for them, too."

"You mean they can become legal refugees?"

"Maybe," he said thoughtfully. "They've been unfairly victimized as large-property owners in their country. They're educated. And good, ordinary citizens."

"It's true. But what really matters is that we can do something to help them," Annie protested angrily. "These women are individuals, people in need. Regardless of their heritage or their past, they deserve a chance."

"You're right, Annie. But everything that has happened to them probably happened because they had some wealth and property. That makes them even more vulnerable now, when they have nothing. It also increases their possibility of being categorized as refugees."

"I never thought of it that way." Annie looked at him sharply. "Then you won't turn them in? You'll help?"

"No, I won't turn them—or you—in. And I'll see what can be done to help."

"Oh, Brett!" She hugged him quickly. "I knew you would!"

He took her shoulders and pushed her back. "Now, hold on. I'm not guaranteeing anything. Sounds to me as though they might qualify, but what do I know about it? And, as for Thomas . . . as Carmen says, *¿quién sabe?* Who knows?"

Annie smiled hopefully. "I trust you to do what's right for them, Brett. I just know you'll be able to help." She pressed herself against him, breathing a sigh of relief and letting her love envelop them.

But after he left, her doubts returned. It had been too easy to convince him, she decided. He was too agreeable, too quickly. Could she *really* trust him?

THERE WAS ANOTHER who did not trust Brett. Not completely. And when dusk covered the landscape with a gray veil, Diego shared his fears with the women. Later that night, under cover of darkness, the three slipped out of the shed. The two women clutched their meager belongings as they huddled together and disappeared into the black night.

11

THE NEXT MORNING WAS welcomingly quiet as Annie puttered about the kitchen, making coffee and warming a bran muffin. She was hovering over her cup of steaming coffee, pinching raisins from the muffin and munching them, when she realized it was too quiet. She usually had company by now. Isabel and Carmen were regulars for breakfast nowadays. In fact, they generally had the coffee going and something prepared that Annie could nibble on by the time she arrived.

Annie found them pleasant company. She would certainly miss them when they left. She glanced at the clock. Eight-thirty. They were *always* here by this time. Wondering if they were all right, she bolted suddenly from her chair to go check on them.

She ran across the yard and dashed into the little room adjoining the shed. The room was vacant. No signs of Isabel and Carmen; no traces of their habitation. Where in the world could they be at this hour of the morning?

Stunned and a little frightened by her discovery, she ran to find Diego. He was checking on the Jonathan orchard today, so she bounded into the truck and headed in that direction.

"Diego! Diego!" Annie called to him even before she turned off the engine. She spotted him halfway down the row, adjusting a sprinkler. She reached him, puffing breathlessly, "They're...gone! Isabel and...Carmen aren't in their room!"

"I know."

She pulled up short. "You know what?"

"That they left, *señorita*," he answered calmly.

"You mean that they're gone for good?"

He nodded.

"You know that for sure? Why didn't you tell me?"

"They wanted their journey to be a secret."

"I know, but I was *in* on their secret. I just can't believe they wouldn't tell me. When did they leave?"

"Sometime in the night."

"Where did they go?"

"*¿Quién sabe?* Who knows?"

Annie was dumbfounded by the news. Isabel and Carmen had actually left to continue on their journey? "Thomas...Thomas came for them?"

"I do not know about him, *señorita*."

"But, Diego, where would they go? I'm sure they wouldn't leave without him. Where has he been all this time?"

Diego shook his head and continued working on the sprinkler head.

Annie felt like crying. She took a few stumbling steps away, trying to adjust to the news. She reached for a branch near her head, absently caressing the tiny green apple growing there. Usually she was so thrilled with the current new crop that it grabbed all her attention. Today, though, she could think only of Isabel and Carmen. Where were they?

She turned back to the truck, crestfallen and disappointed. She told herself she had known all along the women would leave. But so suddenly? And without saying anything, not even . . . goodbye? She was hurt, dammit. Downright hurt.

Annie climbed back into the truck and started the engine. They were gone. And that was that. She should be relieved. No more hiding and worrying. No more tension when Brett was around . . .

At the intersection of the main road, rather than turning back to the house, something quite beyond her understanding compelled her to turn toward Brett's.

Frankly there was no one she would rather be with right now than him. Brett was her friend. Her friend and lover. He cared for her, she knew he did. Even though he had never declared anything so drastic as love, she felt that his affection for her was deep. He knew her darkest secret, that she had defied the law by hiding her refugees. He had met the women and knew her concern for them. She could talk to him, and he would understand her disappointment. She rushed to his porch and pounded on the door. It took him several minutes to open the door.

Brett blinked in the bright morning sunlight. He felt a welcoming flood of intimacy and warmth on seeing Annie. But even in his sleepy stupor, he recognized that she was like a firecracker, ready to explode.

"Hey, Annie. Come in."

"I hope I'm not too early." She could tell that she was. Obviously he had been in bed when she arrived. He wore cutoff jeans, and nothing else. His broad, bare chest revealed the richly textured, tanned skin that she loved to touch. The fringed pant legs circled his muscular thighs, reminding her of the sexy way those legs felt next to hers.

"Of course not. I'm always here for you."

"You were still in bed."

"I worked late last night. Caught another bunch bringing aliens in from Mexico."

"Sorry, Brett. I . . . I just wanted to talk."

"Are you all right, Annie?"

That was all she needed. The tears hovering near the surface spilled over and rolled down her cheeks.

And that was all Brett needed! Seeing Annie cry tore him apart. He wrapped her in his arms and cuddled her against his chest. Gently he led her into the living room. "What's wrong, my dear, sweet Annie? Are you okay? Is Diego?" When she nodded mutely, he continued. "What about the women? The . . . uh, refugees?"

She sniffled and wiped the tears, shaking her head. "They're gone."

"Well, aren't you a little bit glad?"

"They didn't even say goodbye."

"Ungrateful people."

"No. That isn't like them. Not at all. I can't figure what happened."

"When did they leave?"

"Sometime in the night. They just didn't show up this morning."

"Did the husband arrive? What's his name? Thomas?"

"No. At least, I didn't know if he did."

"Did they say they were leaving? Or give some warning?"

"No. Nothing."

"Then how do you know they left? Maybe they just went for a walk."

"Their things are gone from their room. Cleared out completely. And when I asked Diego about them, he said they were gone. And they wanted to keep it a secret."

Brett shrugged. "Well, I can understand that."

"But I was a part of their secret. I risked a lot to help them. And to keep them hidden. The least they could do was to let me know when they were leaving." Her disappointment was evolving into anger. "Dammit, Brett, they could have said thanks, or . . . goodbye."

"Sounds reasonable. But maybe they were too afraid."

"Of what? Me?" She scoffed. "I'm the one who saved them. I'm the one who—" She slammed her palm down onto her thigh. "It just isn't like them to do this."

"Well, when I'm investigating something and someone says, 'it isn't like them to do this,' I look for further clues. Sometimes there are other reasons. But other times, there's trouble."

"You mean, foul play?" Annie's eyes rounded as she said the words. "Oh, Brett, you don't think—"

"No, I don't think anything yet. I'm just saying that there may be other circumstances. According to you, some things just don't figure with these two. Like leaving without saying goodbye."

She nodded emphatically. "Last weekend, when you and I went to Tucson and left them, we said our goodbyes, thinking there was a possibility that Thomas would come and want them to leave right away. But, I think that all three of us were hoping it wouldn't happen until I returned. That's why Carmen met me at the car with a hug. She was so happy to see me again."

"And it isn't like them to be ungrateful or—" he shrugged "—simply negligent?"

"Not at all! They have been grateful for every little thing I ever did for them. They were constantly thanking me in various ways by doing chores around the farm." Annie shook her head. "I can't imagine them leaving like this, even if Thomas came unexpectedly."

"But you don't know for sure that he did?"

"No."

"That seems odd, too, since everyone, including you, has been so concerned about his welfare."

"They knew I cared about them and Thomas. And...the baby." She frowned. "You know, Brett, I don't know much about pregnant women and babies, but Carmen looked so weary lately. And she's pretty big. She could be further along than she claims. And I wonder...if she's all right."

He squeezed her hand. "Now, don't worry about that. I'm sure she is. You say that Diego is the only one who knows that they left?"

She nodded.

"Why would they let him know, and not you?"

"Well, he's been in on it from the start. He knew about them when they first hid in the mission ruins."

"Still, seems strange that he's the only one who knows."

They sat quietly for a few minutes. Then, their eyes met.

"Let's go talk with Diego," Brett suggested gently.

"You don't think he's involved in this, do you?"

"I don't know what to think at this point, Annie. But I'll bet we can get more answers from him than we now have. Give me a minute to change clothes."

ANNIE STOOD BACK quietly while Brett grilled Diego. But all he got from the old man was, "I don't know."

"He's very clever," Brett admitted to Annie later as she prepared them a chicken sandwich for lunch. "But he's lying."

The plate clattered to the table from Annie's nervous hand. "Why would he do that?"

"I don't know. But I intend to find out."

Annie sat opposite him. "I can't believe Diego would lie to me."

"Maybe he did it out of fear for your safety."

"*My* safety? From what?"

"Well, the longer you kept them, the greater your risk of getting caught. Maybe he felt guilty for getting you involved."

"But why doesn't he just say so?"

"He doesn't want to admit anything. Like where they are right now."

"You think they're still around?"

"I think it's unlikely that Thomas showed up so suddenly, and they disappeared so quickly."

"So do I. But where could they be? Brett, you don't think Diego's done something with them, do you? Maybe hidden them somewhere else?" She shook her head as if to answer her own question. "That's ridiculous. Why would he do that?"

"You tell me. Was he overly protective of them?"

"Yes, sort of. In the beginning, he practically begged me to help them when Isabel was sick."

"Maybe he felt threatened by something."

She studied the sandwich before her. "The only thing I did was to introduce them to you."

He snapped his fingers. "That's it! He doesn't trust me on something so close to the arm of the law."

"Why, Brett, you've never given him any reason not to trust you."

"I also haven't given him any reason to trust me. And for something like this, he would need proof that I could be trusted. I understand that reasoning."

"But why would he hurt me like this by taking them so suddenly?"

"I don't think he knew it would hurt you."

"What does he think I'm made of? Steel?"

"Frankly, darling," Brett said softly. "I don't think he considered your feelings here. Or he wouldn't have done it quite like this."

"So what are we going to do?"

Brett looked into her eyes. "We're going to find them."

"Oh, Brett—" She rose from the table and went to him. "I love you," she whispered as she wound her arms around his neck and squeezed him to her. "Thank you! Thank you for understanding how I feel. For caring!"

Brett's arms enfolded her, pressing her close to his body. Oh, yes, he understood. Annie had a way from the beginning of making him understand. And caring. Oh, Lord, did he ever care for this woman! Far too much. And far beyond his control.

BRETT DROVE HER TRUCK. Annie sat beside him quietly, hands pressed together in her lap. She was worried, but she trusted him. He could see that trust in her eyes. How could he betray them? Still, as he drove in search of the refugees, he figured he must be absolutely crazy.

No, not literally crazy. Just crazy about one beautiful lady in tight blue jeans with wild strawberry hair and green eyes that mesmerized him into doing her bidding. Eyes that he couldn't resist. Eyes that he couldn't disappoint.

"Where're we going?"

"I think I know where they might be. Or who might know where they are."

"Why are you doing this, Brett?"

"Beats me. It's absolutely crazy."

"Then, don't. It would look very bad for you if someone knew what you were doing. You could even . . . lose your job. Please, let me search alone."

He took her hand and pressed it to his lips. "Can't do that, Annie. I just can't." Oh, how he wished he could. She was right. This was risky for him. And yet he hadn't even thought of it until she mentioned it. He could only think of the torment of the lady beside him. And what he could do to relieve that frown from her beautiful brow and those heavy sighs from her sensuous lips.

His lips played along her knuckles, kissing, silently promising that everything would be all right.

Annie leaned her shoulder against his. She had always been aware that Brett was strong, but now he was revealing even greater strength by risking everything for her. She would never forget it. Or him.

They turned into the parking lot of the familiar white-frame building that housed Dr. Theresa's small clinic. Brett parked under the tree near the back door. "Wait here. I'll be right back."

"Dr. Theresa?"

"Sh. Don't speculate. She may know something, that's all."

Annie waited for the longest twenty minutes of her life. She was anxious and tempted to follow Brett. But she knew that wouldn't help. Dr. Theresa was busy. And Brett could certainly find out more from his old friend without Annie there. Still, it was hard to wait.

When he finally bounded out the door and down the steps, he wore a grim expression. Annie knew, even before he hopped into the truck, that he had not received the answers he wanted.

"Nothing?" she asked with disappointment in her voice.

"Not from Theresa. But she gave me a good lead."

Annie looked at him curiously. "Oh? Where?"

"Roman."

"Roman? Lacy and Holt's foster son?"

"Yep."

After consulting with the youth for the better part of an hour, Brett convinced him they meant no harm to the refugees. Annie knew that Brett's hero status with Roman hadn't hurt. Still, Roman was a sensible young man who recognized potential trouble when he saw it. And Carmen's advanced state of pregnancy had not gone unnoticed.

Quietly he climbed into the truck with Brett and Annie and pointed them out of town.

"Why did you do this, Roman?" Annie asked as they headed toward the foothills north of town.

"Hey, just to help out, you know? Diego asked me if I could help. Said it was a matter of life and death. Is that so? Are these women on the lam?"

"Well, not exactly," Annie said. "But they are hiding from the sheriff. They're refugees from Nicaragua. And they're very scared."

"Yeah. Scared of everything." Roman pointed for Brett to turn left onto a dirt road. "Hey, the one chick who's going to be a mama soon, she is very big. That one kind of scared me. I mean, I thought whoa! What if—you know?"

"How much farther?"

"Not much." He gestured toward a clump of mesquite trees that gathered around and almost hid a shack in the distance.

"Over there."

"How did you know about this place, Roman?" Annie strained to see the building. There were no signs of life. Well, what did she expect? They were hiding.

"Aw, I found it one time when I needed a place."

Annie remembered Lacy recounting how Roman and his little sister had lived somewhere on their own until they were discovered to have no home and no guardians. This must have been the place.

Brett pulled to a stop near the shack. "You go in first, Roman," he instructed. "Tell them Annie's here. And that I'm here, and I can be trusted. Tell them everything's going to be all right. No one is going to turn them in, but they really should see Annie. Go on, now."

Roman nodded. He knew what he had to do. Slowly he left the truck and made his way to the shack. He knocked, then slipped inside the rickety building.

Annie looked at Brett. "Should I go, too? They must be pretty scared by now."

"Probably wouldn't hurt. They trust you."

At that moment, they heard a shout. They looked up to see Roman standing midway between the truck and the shack. He waved for them. "Yo, Annie! Com'ere quick!"

Annie was out of the truck in a flash. "What is it?"

"Hey, something's happening with the little mother!"

"Oh, my Lord!" Annie preceded him inside the semi-dark building. The room was hot and stuffy.

Carmen lay on a makeshift bed, groaning. She was obviously in labor. Isabel stood near her side, making soft, encouraging noises in Spanish.

"Isabel, Carmen...it's me." Annie slipped past the older woman and took Carmen's hand. "*¿Qué pasa?* What's happening?"

The young woman looked up at Annie, the fear in her eyes mingling with relief, and she smiled faintly. She squeezed Annie's hand until the pain was over.

"Carmen, oh, dear Carmen, we're going to get you out of here." She pushed Carmen's sweat-drenched hair off her forehead. "Everything's going to be all right."

Annie turned to Brett. "Do something! She's having the baby!"

12

"Do something?" Brett almost laughed. But the situation was too serious.

He surveyed the scene before him. Annie silently pleaded with him, *do something* written all over her stricken face. Isabel hovered over Carmen, resting her hand on the younger woman's tight belly, speaking quietly to her in Spanish. Carmen's eyes were wide with the fright of a woman caught in circumstances beyond her control.

The only one in the room who seemed calm was Isabel. And in this moment of crisis, Brett realized it was crucial for a calm attitude to be relayed to Carmen. She was having a baby. And she needed to feel that everything around her was stable, that the people surrounding her were in control of whatever might happen. And most of all, that her baby would be all right.

So, as he had done many times, under much different circumstances, Brett took control.

"Isabel, *por favor*, talk to me." He took her arm and led her away from Carmen's hearing. "How long has she been in labor?"

"No much," Isabel answered in her broken English.

Brett tried another tactic. "How many labor pains has she had today? *¿Cuánto? ¿Dos o diez?* Two or ten?"

Isabel shrugged. *"Dos o tres."*

"Two or three? Good. Then she's just starting labor. And since it's her first, we probably have time to take her to Dr. Theresa's clinic. Do you think so?"

Isabel nodded, relief in her tired eyes. "Ah, *sí*. Dr. Theresa, *sí*."

"Okay, people, listen up! We have to work together here." Brett's voice assumed an authoritarian tone as he began to issue orders. "We're going to move Carmen to Dr. Theresa's clinic. She'll be safer there. And so will the baby. She isn't far into labor, and I think we have plenty of time. *If* we hurry."

Annie nodded to Brett, then gave Roman a tight, reassuring smile. The boy looked a little stunned. "Sounds like a good idea. What do you want us to do, Brett?"

"We're going to move Carmen's bed to the back of the truck and transport her that way."

"Okay." Annie helped Carmen to her feet and, with Isabel on her other side, walked her slowly across the room.

Meantime, Brett and Roman quickly started hauling the mattress across the room. Suddenly Carmen cried out with another pain. Isabel and Annie struggled to keep her from falling to the floor.

Brett immediately swept the bulky, writhing woman into his arms. "We've got to hurry. Her pains are coming too close together. Annie, you and Roman get that mattress to the truck. *Quick!* Isabel, get the blanket. *Pronto!*"

Everyone swung into action. There was no more time to be scared, to stand around wondering what to do next. It was happening fast. And they had to do what was necessary or that baby would be born here in this hovel. And no one wanted that to happen.

Exhibiting the utmost care, Brett cradled Carmen and lifted her swollen body to the makeshift bed in the back of Annie's old truck. Isabel and Annie crawled in beside Carmen while Roman sat in the cab with Brett. With a grim set to his mouth, he drove steadily over the dirt road, trying to speed, yet still avoid the potholes and ruts. Roman, using his usual crafty knowledge, showed Brett a shortcut around town that led direct to Dr. Theresa's. By the time they arrived, Carmen's pains were coming every few minutes.

Annie dashed inside to get the doctor while Brett and Roman attempted to get the woman out of the truck. They scooted the mattress and Carmen to the edge of the truck bed. Brett hopped to the ground and prepared to lift Carmen.

"Wait!" cried Dr. Theresa, pushing Brett aside. "Let me check her before you move her."

For a moment, the only sound came from Carmen. Her low moans changed to heavy, deep breaths, then a panting sound.

"Oh, Lord," Annie murmured to Brett.

"I think we barely got here in time," he whispered.

"She's having it now," Dr. Theresa announced in a steady tone. "We'll just leave her here."

"Yo, man," Roman said. "I'm outta here!"

"No, I need you. All of you," Dr. Theresa commanded. "Roman, go to the pharmacy next door and tell Manny what's happening out here. He'll know what to bring. Quick!"

Roman took off in a run.

"Annie, clean sheets are in the cabinet inside the back door. Get as many as you can carry. And my black bag is, uh, on my desk, I think. Go help her, Isabel. Hurry, now! We're going to have a baby in a few minutes here, and I want something clean around the area."

Annie and Isabel scurried into the clinic.

"Brett, climb up into the truck and kneel at her head. I want you to help Carmen lift her shoulders when I tell you." Dr. Theresa gave Carmen a reassuring pat and a confident smile. "Now, Carmen, everything's moving along as it should. You're going to have a little baby soon. Here's what I want you to do. . . ."

And so, from the back of Annie's truck, with assistance from an anxious group of friends, Dr. Theresa delivered Carmen's baby. The high-pitched infant's cry was the most joyous sound in the world, and all responded with relieved laughter and hugs.

Dr. Theresa calmly wrapped the newborn in a clean sheet and handed the tiny bundle to Isabel. "Your new grandson, Isabel. He's a U.S. citizen by birthright."

The new grandmother gazed at the baby with instant love. She looked up at Dr. Theresa, then at Annie, her wrinkled face beaming with a most beautiful smile. "*Gracias, gracias, gracias a dios*," she murmured repeatedly.

"Take the baby inside so I can examine him," Dr. Theresa said, gathering some of her equipment and heading for the clinic's back door. "Okay, Brett, you and Manny carry Carmen inside. Careful, now. You help, too, Roman. You've been a part of this. May as well finish."

"Whoa, man," he said, stretching to view the baby in Isabel's arms. "A brand-new dude. I've seen everything now!"

Brett caught Annie's gaze and winked. His expression said more than mere words could. In those beautiful dark eyes of his, she saw relief, caring and, most of all, love. For the moment, her heart sang with joy.

IT WAS EARLY EVENING before Annie and Brett could relax in her kitchen. They left Carmen and the new baby in Dr. Theresa's care, took Roman home and brought Isabel back to the apple farm.

Brett was just hanging up the phone as Annie returned from getting Isabel settled back in Diego's room. "Theresa says the baby's okay, but a bit small. Probably a few weeks' premature. She wants to keep an eye on him a few days. Meantime, Carmen is resting and doing fine."

"Great." Annie heaved a sigh and sank into the nearest chair. Gratefully she took a big gulp from the tall glass of iced tea Brett handed her. "Isabel has calmed down enough to rest, I hope. She's been pretty excited by all the events of the day. And last night." She shook her head. "I can't believe all that's happened in the past twenty-four hours."

"For a sleepy little town, this one has lots of activity."

She grinned. "I keep telling you, we're on our way to being a metropolis."

Brett laughed. "Silverton has a ways to go before it's classified as a bustling city, but it's not doing badly."

"Actually, I think most of us would be satisfied with thriving-town status." Annie paused for another long drink. "You know, Brett, I couldn't find Diego. I have no idea where he is."

"Probably skipped out," Brett muttered, his tone revealing his agitation with the old man. "Damn fool probably brought all this on Carmen by hauling those women out in the country like that."

Annie wasn't so quick to place blame on the old man. "I'm sure he had no idea that he was creating such problems—if that's really the case."

"He didn't think it through, that's for sure. If only I'd had a car phone," Brett said, pacing the floor. "We could have contacted an ambulance for Carmen."

"Actually, Dr. Theresa's clinic was closer than the hospital. And I thought we made it as fast as any ambulance could have."

"Then we could've called the paramedics. We came damn close to delivering that baby ourselves. Too close!"

"Silverton doesn't have any paramedics."

"It should. What if you have a bigger emergency than this?"

"Good point. That takes money, though, and we're still struggling."

"You need to get your priorities straight! Emergency and fire service is crucial."

"You're right, Brett." She stood and faced him, hands on her hips. "Why don't you pretend Silverton is your town and present that proposal, along with a funding method, to the next city council meeting."

"I just might do that."

She angled her head and looked at him curiously. "Which? Pretend Silverton's your town? Or make the presentation?"

His gaze enveloped her. "Both." He reached for her, hauling her roughly into his arms. "It's been a helluva day, and I've been wanting to do this for hours." His lips captured hers in a sweet, fervent kiss that expressed joy and caring and passion.

And, Annie hoped with all her heart, love.

"I didn't mean to be so sharp," he murmured. "I'm just edgy. And tired."

"Thanks for going with me to look for them today," she returned with understanding in her tone. She remembered that he had worked last night and she had gotten him up early. "And for finding them. What you did took a tremendous amount of courage."

"No, it didn't. How could I look into your eyes, Annie, and refuse you anything?"

She smiled, wondering if she asked for love, would he give it? Would he admit it? But she couldn't ask. Love was something that had to be given freely. "If you hadn't used your sources to find them, Carmen would have had her baby in that shack, with only poor Isabel in attendance. And anything might have happened. They might not have survived—"

"Don't torment yourself with what-ifs. We made it in time. And that's all that counts."

She rested her cheek on his chest. "I was so proud of you today, Brett. When I first saw Carmen and realized her condition, I was scared. But you were magnificent. Just like a hero—"

He stiffened. "Don't say it, Annie. I simply did what had to be done. We all did our share. Including Roman."

They heard a scuffing noise on the back porch and the clearing of a throat.

Annie slipped out of Brett's embrace. "Diego? Diego! Where have you been?" She went to the porch and motioned. "Come on in. I want to talk to you."

After a moment, the old man shuffled into the kitchen.

Brett sat down, wisely deciding to keep out of this. He was so angry that he might say or do the wrong thing. Annie was much more diplomatic. Anyway, Diego was her manager.

"Where have you been?" Annie demanded.

"At the old mission ruins."

"Hiding?"

Diego shrugged. He held his hat in front with both hands.

"I was worried about you, Diego. While you were out there hiding, we were taking Carmen to the clinic."

His eyes widened. "She is ill?"

"She had her baby, Diego. They're fine, now, but we had a devil of a time finding them. Whatever, in your wildest thoughts, made you take them away from here?"

"I wanted them to be safe."

"They were safe here."

"But not after the . . . uh, law found them."

"You mean, Brett?"

He shrugged again, avoiding eye contact with either her or Brett. "You never know. Anyway, things were going to happen. And I wanted them away from here. Away from you."

"Things? What things?"

"Thomas."

"Carmen's husband?" Annie asked, excitement creeping into her voice.

Diego nodded. "I heard that he was on his way soon. And I was afraid that whatever happened would be bad for you. The sheriff would think that you are harboring aliens. I did not want that."

"Oh, Diego, I appreciate your concern, but I'm not worried about that anymore. I believe they're refugees. And, as for Brett—" she smiled at him, "—after what he did for Carmen today, there's no doubt that he can be trusted to keep our secret. Anyway, we want to see Thomas arrive safely. He has a son now."

"Thomas . . . he . . ." Diego stopped and glanced anxiously at Brett.

"What, Diego?" Brett asked. "Is he all right?"

"He is at the mission."

"The ruins?" Annie pressed her hand to her mouth and released a cry of joy.

"How did he get there?" Brett jumped to his feet. "Is he okay?"

Diego looked from one to the other, a little frightened at their reactions to the new information he had just imparted. "He is waiting for his family."

"Diego, just to show you that I can be trusted, let's go escort Thomas to the clinic!" Brett clapped his arm around old Diego's shoulder. "The man has a son!"

"First," Annie suggested gently, "take him to see his mother, Isabel. It would make her day complete. Then, bring him back here for some *pozole*. I'm sure he's hungry."

"I know *we* sure are, huh, Diego?" Brett gave her a little wave as they headed out the door.

MORE THAN TWO WEEKS LATER, the little refugee family was ready to leave. Sad though she was to see them go, Annie knew they would be better off in their new home. Dr. Theresa had contacted a California group willing to receive them and help them attain U.S. citizenship and begin their new lives.

Brett made arrangements for their safe passage west.

Annie sent them off loaded with food, including several loaves of apple bread and a large bag of freshly picked apples from the new crop. With teary eyes, Annie bid them farewell and made Carmen promise to call or write regularly and let her know how things were going and, especially, about baby Diego Thomas Allende.

When the transporting van disappeared, Brett hugged her shoulders. "They're going to be just fine, Annie."

"I hope so."

"They are. Thomas is smart and very capable. He made it out of his country and through heaven-knows-what in Mexico, didn't he? With the help of the California Refugee League, he'll certainly make it in this country."

Annie spread the embroidered cloth Isabel had presented to her as a gift. "I'll always have this to remind me of them."

"What is it?"

"It's a church altar cloth," she explained. "This is the special colcha embroidery Isabel was working on while they waited on Thomas."

"Oh, yes. It's the kind my grandmother used to make." He admired the precise threads weaving a colorful design along the material. "It's almost a lost art."

"Maybe this piece should go in the folk art museum," Annie suggested. "It's a fine example of colcha embroidery. But also, it's a reminder of some remarkable people who passed this way once."

"Only once," he repeated. "No more, Annie. Understand? No more refugees hiding on your farm."

"Right." She grinned up at him. "Did I ever thank you for everything you did to help?"

"About a dozen times."

"Here's a dozen and one." She stood on tiptoe and kissed his lips. Then, arm in arm, they walked back to the house. "I guess," she said softly in her melancholy mood, "I guess you're next."

"Next for what?"

"To leave."

He halted and turned her in his arms. "Whatever gave you that idea?"

She shrugged. "The work is done. The apples are ready to be harvested, and I can hire migrants for that. You saved the farm and the refugees. Time for the white-hatted hero to get on his horse and ride off into the sunset."

"That's ridiculous! What gave you the idea that I would leave now, after all that's happened? All we've meant to each other? I could never leave you, Annie. I love you."

He looked as shocked by his words as she did.

Annie recovered first. "I don't want you to stay here because of me, Brett. I don't want to be blamed when things don't work out. Or you get bored."

His arms circled her and pulled her closer. "I love you with all my heart, Annie. How can I convince you of that?" His lips settled on hers, kissing her with such passion that he took her breath away.

Annie succumbed to his kiss and let it speak for him. There was nothing else to say. For the moment, he loved her. She couldn't, however, tell him how she could be convinced.

But Brett already knew. He not only had to tell Annie of his love, he had to prove it. And he set to doing just that. It took him about two weeks to do what was necessary.

ANNIE WALKED AMONG the familiar ruins. The late summer weeds were knee-high and filled what was once the church sanctuary. She stepped onto a large stone in front of the mission and surveyed the nearest orchard. Migrant workers had nearly picked it clean today. A sense of pride swelled in her breast.

"It's a good crop, Aunt Annalee," she said aloud. "I've been busy harvesting during the day. And at night I bake pies and apple bread, just like you used to do. Silverton's fall fiesta isn't far away. It's going to be wonderful. We've invited mariachis from Tucson."

She hopped down and continued her walk. "I heard from Carmen today. They're living with a nice family in California until Thomas can get a job and make enough money for them to live alone. The baby's fine." She smiled wistfully. "I miss them."

Annie sat on a low brick wall. She felt the day's warmth radiate from the bricks into her body. "I haven't seen much of Brett lately. He claimed he loved me. He said it once. But I think he's getting ready to leave. After all, it's pretty dull and boring around here now that Carmen and Isabel are gone. No more excitement."

She looked up at the sound of an engine. A shiny red truck with large silver spotlights above the windshield and a fancy antenna on the roof parked behind her old

Jeep. When the door of the unfamiliar pickup opened, Brett emerged.

Brett? Annie stood up and curiously watched the lean-hipped, broad-shouldered figure come toward her. He was every bit as handsome as the first day she saw him. And the sight of him still made her heart pound and her stomach jittery.

He looked, somehow, different. Today he wore jeans and a pale blue shirt opened at the neck. With dirty white tennis shoes. No shiny boots. And he wore an appealing little half grin that drove her crazy. What was he up to, anyway?

"Hey, Annie. Want to ride in my new truck?"

"Your truck? Got a new toy, Brett?" She cast another glance at the contrasting vehicles. His was, of course, as spiffy a truck as she had ever seen. Her Jeep was still a rattletrap.

"It's a four-wheel hoss. Got the works, too. Just drove it in from Albuquerque."

She raised her eyebrows. So that was where he'd been the past two days.

"I traded my car for it," he continued, taking her hand. "Come on, Annie. Let me show you."

She looked up curiously. "You traded the Mercedes?"

"You catch on slow." He led her to the fancy truck and showed her all the bells and whistles. It even had a telephone. "Want to make a call?"

Annie shook her head. "Not right now, thanks."

"It has a police radio, spotlights, phone, stereo, automatic-everything that I need in my work."

"Need?"

"You bet! I can't be out in the middle of nowhere, needing a backup or to make contact with civilization. This way, I could even call you and tell you I'll be late for supper." He started the big engine, which purred like a giant cat. "Wait'll you see how this baby runs."

The ride was almost—not quite, but almost—as smooth as the Mercedes'. They drove to the Rocking M, where Brett ushered her in the front door of his old homestead. The living room was completely repaired and freshly painted. The rug had been pulled up and rich red tile covered the floor.

"Don't have the furniture yet, but I figured you could help pick it out." He stopped by the little bedroom that used to be his, the room where they had made love. It was obvious that he no longer slept in there. "It's really for a kid, don't you think?" He steered her to the kitchen. "Hope you like it."

Annie gasped with delight. The kitchen was clean and painted and usable again. "It's wonderful! Did you do all this? How? When?"

"I had a little help," he admitted with a grin. "From Roman and Holt."

"And they kept it a secret from me?"

"Of course. Wait till you see the master bedroom." He took her hand.

They went to the back bedroom, a room that Annie had never seen. She walked in hesitantly. This was where Brett's parents had made love. The large bed was made of heavy oak and covered with an old-fashioned crocheted bedspread.

"My mom made it. But if you want something different, I understand."

"Oh, Brett . . ." Annie felt as if she were entering an enchanted castle. "It's beautiful."

"At first I felt funny when I saw this room looking exactly as my folks had it. But now, I think it's just the way it should be. Sort of traditional."

Annie walked into the center of the room and turned to face him. "Why are you showing me this?"

Brett's face was tight, but he continued. "The bedspread has been packed away for years. I figured it was time to make this place a home again. To use the master bedroom as it was meant to be, for adults. To follow tradition and . . . make a few of my own." He moved before her and took her hands. "But I need a wife for that, Annie. And I want you to be the one."

Annie's voice stuck in her throat. She felt as if she had been thrown onto a merry-go-round from the moment he tucked her into the shiny red truck. The house was so different, and in some ways, so was Brett. And yet, he was still the same man with whom she had fallen in love.

She was barely aware that he was kissing her, his lips tantalizing her shocked senses. Annie clung to his shoulders, weakly wondering if she was dreaming. Or if any part of this was real.

"There's more, Annie," he said through the thick veil of fog that seemed to shroud her. They walked to the back patio. From there they could see into a nearby field. "My first few head of cattle," he said proudly.

She shielded her eyes and squinted. "Cattle, Brett?"

He shrugged. "I'm going to try my hand at ranching. If I'm no better at it than my dad was, I'll have my teaching and law enforcement work with the sheriff's department to fall back on."

She laughed aloud. It was too good to be true. It *was* a dream! "You've done all this, Brett? Why?"

"Only one reason, Annie. To prove that I love you. That I'm ready to settle down. And I'll never leave you." He pulled her into his embrace. "I love you more than I ever thought possible."

She looked up into his serious brown eyes. "I love you, too, Brett. I loved you from the start. But all along, I was afraid that I was throwing my love away. I thought . . . that you'd leave, like everyone else I've ever loved."

"I'll never leave you, Annie. I promise."

His kiss sealed the promise with warm passion. When he raised his head, lights danced in his dark eyes. "I'd like to have a party. For our friends and family . . . to announce our engagement. That is, if you'll be my bride."

Her face shining with happiness, Annie looked up at him. "I can't believe this is happening, Brett. It's everything I ever wanted. It's like a dream come true."

He framed her face with his large tanned hands. "You're everything I ever wanted. Say you'll marry me, Annie." He kissed her lips lightly.

"Yes . . ." she murmured.

The kiss that followed led to more kisses and . . . much more. Later they watched the sunset from the patio, overlooking the field with five cows feeding on the scrubby grass. They would be the new herd of the Rocking M Cattle Ranch.

"What about the apple farm?"

"We'll figure out a merger, after the wedding. Basically though, I feel that the farm is your property, Annie. I don't want to destroy that. Anyway, you're building a reputation for the best apples and best apple bread in the county." He lifted her hand and kissed it. "When do you want to get married?"

"I . . . I don't know. But I would like to have our wedding at the old mission ruins," she said tentatively. "We can clean it up, trim the weeds. It's like a garden to me. You don't mind *los espíritus*, do you?"

"Not at all, if they don't mind me." He chuckled and added, "We'll have mariachis."

"And children to dance and sing."

"And J.M. can be my best man. He'd like that."

"Is that a touch of sentiment I hear?"

"Yeah. Tough but sentimental . . ."

"Like father, like son . . ."

"And we can use the colcha embroidery altar cloth. Then when you donate it to the museum, it'll have double sentiment."

"How sweet," she murmured. Suddenly she sat up and looked at him. "Are you sure you want to do this, Brett? To settle down in boring Silverton?"

"How could anyone be bored around you, Annie? Life is always exciting." He tousled her hair. "Risky, but exciting."

Teasingly she mussed his neat black hair. "As exciting as watching apples grow?"

"You, my dear lovable Annie, are all the excitement I need for a lifetime."

Brett held Annie in his arms and kissed her until the sun set behind the old mission ruins. He would spend a lifetime proving his love.

And Annie . . . she spent a lifetime loving Brett and sharing the excitement of watching their apples and their children grow.

COMING NEXT MONTH

#297 HAVING FAITH Barbara Delinsky

Faith Barry knew making love with Sawyer Bell had been a
big mistake. He was an old, dear friend *and* they were
representing opposing clients in a complicated divorce case.
But they had crossed that line between lovers and friends.
Now Faith faced a new dilemma—how to keep the
courtroom battle out of the bedroom....

#298 GOING, GOING, GONE!
Bess Shannon

Constance Nathan, VP of a prestigious auction house, had
been appointed to appraise the late Marquise de Vernay's
possessions. So had art-museum curator Kenneth
Considine. Connie thought she was armed for the duel:
whatever wasn't retained for the museum, she would
catalog for auction. Parrying Ken's insolent charm was her
toughest challenge—until he agreed to a *special* kind
of compromise....

#299 CHANGING THE RULES
Gina Wilkins

It wasn't supposed to happen. Elise Webber and Dustin
Chandler, the fastest of fast-track yuppies in Atlanta, were
about to become parents. Marriage was out of the question
for Elise—they were barely out of the dating phase. But
Dustin was determined to do the honorable thing...even if
he wasn't quite sure just what that was!

#300 ISLAND NIGHTS Glenda Sanders

Janet Granville's Barbados vacation had surpassed her
wildest dreams. She'd met a gorgeous man, and now
Stephen Dumont wanted to marry her—right there on the
island. But it was all too fast for Janet, and she was hesitant
to accept. Could a breathtaking week of fantasy turn into a
lifetime of love?

In April, Harlequin brings you the
world's most popular romance author

JANET DAILEY

No Quarter Asked

Out of print since 1974!

After the tragic death of her father, Stacy's world is shattered. She
needs to get away by herself to sort things out. She leaves behind
her boyfriend, Carter Price, who wants to marry her. However, as
soon as she arrives at her rented cabin in Texas, Cord Harris, owner
of a large ranch, seems determined to get her to leave. When Stacy
has a fall and is injured, Cord reluctantly takes her to his own ranch.
Unknown to Stacy, Carter's father has written to Cord and asked
him to keep an eye on Stacy and try to convince her to return home.
After a few weeks there, in spite of Cord's hateful treatment that
involves her working as a ranch hand and the return of Lydia, his ex-
fiancée, by the time Carter comes to escort her back, Stacy knows
that she is in love with Cord and doesn't want to go.

**Watch for *Fiesta San Antonio* in July and
For Bitter or Worse in September.**

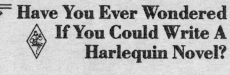

Have You Ever Wondered If You Could Write A Harlequin Novel?

Here's great news—Harlequin is offering a series of cassette tapes to help you do just that. Written by Harlequin editors, these tapes give practical advice on how to make your characters—and your story—come alive. There's a tape for each contemporary romance series Harlequin publishes.

Mail order only

All sales final

TO: **Harlequin Reader Service**
Audiocassette Tape Offer
P.O. Box 1396
Buffalo, NY   14269-1396

I enclose a check/money order payable to HARLEQUIN READER SERVICE® for $9.70 ($8.95 plus 75¢ postage and handling) for EACH tape ordered for the total sum of $＿＿＿＿＿＿*
Please send:

☐ Romance and Presents   ☐ Intrigue
☐ American Romance   ☐ Temptation
☐ Superromance   ☐ All five tapes ($38.80 total)

Signature＿＿＿＿＿＿＿＿＿＿＿＿＿＿＿＿＿＿＿＿＿＿＿＿＿＿
Name:＿＿＿＿＿＿＿＿＿＿＿＿＿＿＿＿＿＿ (please print clearly)

Address:＿＿＿＿＿＿＿＿＿＿＿＿＿＿＿＿＿＿＿＿＿＿＿＿＿＿

State:＿＿＿＿＿＿＿＿＿＿＿＿＿＿   Zip:＿＿＿＿＿＿＿＿＿

*Iowa and New York residents add appropriate sales tax.

AUDIO-H

The Adventurer
JAYNE ANN KRENTZ

Remember THE PIRATE (Temptation #287), the first book
Jayne Ann Krentz's exciting trilogy Ladies and Legends? Ne
month Jayne brings us another powerful romance, TH
ADVENTURER (Temptation #293), in which Kate, Sarah a
Margaret — three long-time friends featured in THE PIRAT
— meet again.

A contemporary version of a great romantic myth, TH
ADVENTURER tells of Sarah Fleetwood's search for lon
lost treasure and for love. Only when she meets her moder
day knight-errant Gideon Trace will Sarah know she's fou
the path to fortune and eternal bliss....

THE ADVENTURER — available in April 1990! And in Jun
look for THE COWBOY (Temptation #302), the third book
this enthralling trilogy.
